A SMALL FORTUNE

When they win the lottery, Angela and Tom leave their roots and move to a designer home overlooking Morecambe Bay. Despite the money, Angela is discontented, and Tom changes — into a businessman with grandiose plans — whilst their daughter Melanie has no aim in life. A visit to Angela's sister, Moira, brings to a head their disparate relationships. Meanwhile, Tom's business plans unravel, bringing unexpected money worries, and Angela faces having to reveal that she's been sending money regularly to Cheryl, a woman who'd sent them a begging letter after the win. Should she trust her? Is Cheryl all she seems?

Books by Patricia Fawcett
Published by The House of Ulverscroft:

SET TO MUSIC
THE ABSENT CHILD
EIGHT DAYS AT THE NEW GRAND
OLIVIA'S GARDEN
THE CUCKOO'S NEST
RETURN TO ROSEMOUNT
EMILY'S WEDDING
FAMILY SECRETS
A PERFECT MOTHER
RUMOURS AND RED ROSES
JUST ANOTHER DAY

SPECIAL MESSAGE TO READERS

THE ULVERSCROFT FOUNDATION
(registered UK charity number 264873)

res   s.

ye

eat

nd
gy,

p,

rn

al

Yo   n

E

v

Leicester LE7 7FU, England
Tel: (0116) 236 4325

website: ft.com

Born in Preston, Lancashire, Patricia Fawcett now lives in Devon, close to her family. She divides her time between writing, being a lively grandmother and a volunteer at a National Trust Property. She is a member of the Romantic Novelists' Association and the West Country Writer's Association. Her previous novels include *Rumours and Red Roses* and *Just Another Day*.

PATRICIA FAWCETT

◆

A SMALL FORTUNE

Complete and Unabridged

ULVERSCROFT
Leicester

First published in Great Britain in 2012 by
Robert Hale Limited
London

First Large Print Edition
published 2013
by arrangement with
Robert Hale Limited
London

A catalogue record for this book is available
from the British Library.

ISBN 978–1–4448–1534–4

Published by
F. A. Thorpe (Publishing)
Anstey, Leicestershire

Set by Words & Graphics Ltd.
Anstey, Leicestershire
Printed and bound in Great Britain by
T. J. International Ltd., Padstow, Cornwall

This book is printed on acid-free paper

To The Also Rans
Quizzers Extraordinaire!

1

Tom Ross was not given to picking up the post in the morning so it was just her luck that on the one day he chose to do it there was a letter from Cheryl Fisher. Angela recognized the pale-blue envelope and the handwriting at once as he handed it to her.

'Who do you know in that neck of the woods?' he asked.

Trust him to have eagle eyes. In seconds he had noticed the postmark.

She hesitated only briefly. 'It's from Adele. I do get occasional letters.'

'Letters? I thought it was all e-mails and texts these days.'

'It's nicer to get a letter.' With a smile she tossed it aside. 'Is there anything else?'

'Nothing important. Pop them in my study, would you?' He glanced at his watch, a hefty platinum Rolex, and drained the rest of his coffee. 'I've got to go. Did you ask Ron to bring the car round?'

'He'll be waiting outside. Where are you off to?'

'I'm going down to Preston. How many times do I have to tell you? I'm meeting Sean.'

'All right. No need to bite my head off.'
She spread a piece of toast with marmalade,
trying not to let his impatience get to her. He
had never talked to her like that back in the
old days but then in the old days, he had
never attended a business meeting either.

'I know I could phone him,' he said,
softening his voice and anticipating her next
question. 'But I do need to see him face to
face. You know what he's like.'

'I know exactly what he's like.' She held
back a sharp comment before she could be
accused of being overly critical. It had all
been said before and a fat lot of good it had
done because Tom had still gone into
business with Sean who must be turning
cartwheels at his luck.

'He never gives me a proper answer on the
phone so I've got to check up on him in
person and see what he's getting up to.'

'When will you be back?'

'Sevenish, but it depends how the meeting
goes. Time means nothing to him and that
office is a shambles. God alone knows what
his secretary does.'

'Knowing Sean, I could hazard a guess,'
she said, unable to avoid the little dig this
time for, unfathomable as it might be, he did
seem able to attract the ladies.

'What the hell is the new wife called?'

'Sophie. Don't get mixed up.'

'I won't. Probably seven then depending on traffic but Sean will expect a two-hour lunch and then if we start going through the figures I'll be there until midnight. You know how much I hate figures.'

'I know. Why don't you ask Charles Grey to check them for you? It's what we pay him for, isn't it? There's no shame, Tom, in admitting you can't add up.'

'It's not as bad as that. Christ, you really know how to give a guy confidence.'

'Sorry.' She smiled, but she saw that she had jolted his pride for his return smile was forced. 'It was just a suggestion to make it easier for you.'

'Thanks then but no thanks. I have to do this myself. I know you don't like Sean but this is business and he's good at it. It's going to be a big success and you're going to be proud of me.'

'I am proud of you already. You don't have to prove anything to me, Tom.'

'Oh yes I do.' He picked up his briefcase before adding that he might have to stay over. 'It's not fair to Ron to have him driving me back late at night. It's a rotten road once we come off the motorway. We'll book in somewhere.'

Angela sensed her husband was avoiding

looking directly at her, guessed the reason why and it was some small consolation that he was feeling guilty.

And so he should. She also wondered what little extra he might be paying Ron to be discreet. She had no idea who the woman was and she wondered if she in turn knew about her. Being a mistress must be a hassle, but it was probably worth her while because of the gifts Tom must be buying for her. She caught sight of the sparkling diamond ring on her finger, loving it of course, but it did tend to overshadow her original more modest engagement ring.

'Have you any plans for today?' he asked, after a moment's painful silence.

'Lunch at The Turret with Barbara Delamere.'

'God help you. See you this evening then. Hopefully. If not, I'll let you know.'

He kissed her goodbye, no doubt already thinking about his meeting or perhaps the later liaison, and then without a backward glance, he was gone.

⋆ ⋆ ⋆

Angela wandered into the hall whose double height windows let in a vast amount of light giving panoramic views of the gardens and

4

the bay beyond. She loved Morecambe Bay with its shallow waters and its deep sands: an expanse of mudflats, channels, tidal pools and the unpredictable quicksands. You had to respect it for it continued year after year to claim lives, the sheer speed of the tide catching people out time and time again.

She watched as Ron held open the passenger door for Tom and, seeing him step into the car she could almost feel that little treacherous lurch of her heart. Ridiculous, of course, but despite his faults, Tom still had a certain power over her which was both maddening and exhilarating.

Things had changed between them, but then that's what happened in a long marriage, ups and downs, peaks and troughs but this present trough was lasting too long. They had both changed and the lottery win had upset the balance of their marriage. Suddenly Tom had become terribly grown-up and serious. He had been carefree once upon a time, enjoying his leisure moments because he worked hard running his painting and decorating business. Angela acted as his unpaid assistant and she also worked part-time over the years at various unde-manding jobs and with just one child and a modest mortgage on their little cottage they managed to keep their heads above water.

Above all, looking back, they were *happy* although of course they did not always realize it, yearning for something better and talking about what they would do if they won the lottery, but then didn't everybody?

At forty-eight he was a handsome man, the man she had married, lean and toned, hanging onto his fairish hair, the blue-eyed boy, his sudden smile — rare these days — every bit as devastating to her as it had always been and she had to face the fact that he was ageing well. He looked equally good in a suit or the sweats which he wore when working out in the area beside the pool.

She did not join him in the daily work-outs. Fortunately, with very little effort she was still the size 12 she had been when they married. It wasn't as if she had let herself go, gained weight, stopped caring. The opposite had happened because she could now afford the costs of high maintenance. Somewhere along the line though she had lost the ability to make *him* go weak at the knees.

He was not the man she had married, the man she had fallen in love with, and she wanted that man back.

Out of the blue recently, he had offered to pay for surgery to tighten up her face, not even realizing when he suggested it that his obvious dissatisfaction with her appearance hit home and hurt her. She refused the offer because not only was she scared stiff of going under the knife but also she had seen some of the women who had succumbed. In any case, she was only forty five and happy with the face she had.

It had knocked her confidence though.

Looking at herself critically, she reckoned she wasn't doing so badly, her shoulder-length dark-brown hair as lustrous as ever. She pushed aside the suspicions she had these days about her husband because it just wasn't worth her while getting into a state about it. If he wanted to leave her he would have done it before now and to be fair to him there had never been any mention of that. There had been that one fling he admitted to years ago, not really a fling as such, more a one-night stand. Since then he had been silent leaving it all to her over-active imagination.

But then that was Tom. She had instantly noticed that twinkle in his eyes when first they met so why shouldn't other women? And now that he had money that was an added attraction. There was that thing with her sister Moira and sometimes even now she caught the look Moira cast Tom's way and wondered if she still had a bit of a hankering for him, but she was married now to Jim, had been for years, and all seemed well with them.

From the window, she watched as Tom settled in the rear of the Jaguar and Ron drove off. Angela felt she should apologize to all and sundry for having a driver for it really was one step too many but it was necessary because Tom had lost his licence last year and there was no way he would allow her to drive him anywhere. There were two reasons for that. He had taught her to drive back in the old days and he still didn't quite trust her to do it competently, and also it would just be too difficult to organize his working life having to rely on her picking him up and dropping him off. He made frequent trips to Sean's office down in Preston and paying Ron to be at his beck and call was the price Tom had to pay for years of excessive speeding; the £30,000 salary was in any case for them a mere drop in the ocean.

Taking the letters through to his study, she put them on the desk — walnut with green leather-lined top — positioned so that he had a wonderful view of the bay in all its changing moods. Their house was nestled in a large plot at the bottom end of the Kent estuary with an unobstructed view across the bay to the town of her birth, not so far as the crow flies but without the bay road bridge — a dream that would never happen — it was a cumbersome drive. They had paid a lot for the plot and yet the sheer size of the interior, the soaring ceiling of the living area, the huge expanse of gleaming wooden floor made Angela uncomfortable and she was not sure she would ever adjust to it. She had always wanted to live on the east shore of the bay but now she was here, perversely and guiltily, she sometimes longed to be back there, standing at the bay's edge on the opposite shore.

Four years on and this expensive house that most people would die for still did not feel like home.

This study or den as their interior designer Megan preferred to call it, was her husband's domain and she rarely set foot in it. Tom spent a lot of time in here working, supposedly in control of his business empire that Angela suspected he knew very little about. He guarded his papers so protectively one would be excused for thinking they were of a highly confidential nature when they were just letters from Sean so full of ridiculous management-speak they might as well be written in code.

The traditional desk sat awkwardly in this room; an abomination according to Megan but Tom had flashed his boyish smile at her and won that one. Tom could do the lot from here, had no need to travel to Preston to see how things were with Sean but that didn't stop him from making the trip two or three times a month and more often than not he stayed over.

He would stay over tonight and she would not question it.

'Have I missed Daddy?' Her daughter was coming from the direction of the pool, rubbing at her damp hair and sweeping past Angela without so much as a smile but then Melanie was not a morning person. Come to think of it she wasn't an afternoon person just now or a night person. She was eighteen and getting too old for her ridiculous moods to be put down to teenage hormones. Angela was surprised to see her up so early but the sunlight filtering through the blinds in her room had probably woken her. An early morning dip in their pool ought to put anyone in a good mood but not necessarily Melanie. She was without a job or a purpose in life and the subject had to be approached sympathetically although that was difficult because Angela was rapidly losing patience.

'Breakfast, love?'

Deciding not to comment about the time for it would be construed as being sarcastic, Angela bustled into the kitchen after her, picking up the discarded towel with which she had been drying her hair. The question was rhetorical because a cup of black coffee was all the girl had and sure enough she shook her head and poured herself a cup before slumping down, her bathrobe gaping open. She was taller than her mother and had inherited her father's long legs. Her toenails were scarlet and a tiny butterfly was tattooed on her ankle. Two months on and Tom still did not know about the tattoo for neither of them had yet plucked up the courage to tell him. Melanie looked younger without make-up but she would not appreciate being told that. She was a pretty girl, would be even prettier if she did not have such a cold, distant air about her.

Angela pulled out a chair and joined her in the eating area. This kitchen was far too white and the random splashes of scarlet, a peculiarity insisted upon by Megan, had the effect of making her think of a bloodied crime scene. Despite the twin ovens, his and hers presumably although that was a laugh, the prospect of actually using this room to prepare and cook food seemed to be an aspect the designer had overlooked. This kitchen was purely for show and Rachel her cleaner kept it pristine to the point of absurdity and sometimes Angela thought of her old comfortable and cluttered kitchen back in the old house with a sort of regret.

'How did the interview go yesterday?'

'Awful. If they think I'm going to get there for eight fifteen every day they can think again. Eight-*fifteen*? I would have to get up at seven to get ready in time. It's the middle of the night.'

'It's not unreasonable. The office staff has to be there before the shop opens.' She helped herself to another coffee, not because she wanted one but because she needed to try to talk some sense into this spoilt child. Where had they gone wrong? It was obvious, of course, stemming from the moment they took her away from all her friends, built this house and switched her, aged thirteen, to the nearby private school, miles in both distance and expectation from her previous comprehensive. 'You'll get used to it, sweetheart, and it's not just office work, it's a management scheme.'

'Management scheme?' Melanie laughed. 'You talk as if it's Marks and Spencer. It's only a crappy little store in a crappy little town.'

'Don't call it that,' she said sharply. 'It's a little goldmine and they have a lovely café now on the top floor.'

'Lovely little café? You are joking? The whole store is stuck in the fifties. It's dying on its feet. It needs new ideas and some young

12

people on the staff.'

Angela raised her eyebrows. Did Melanie realize what she had just said? 'Perhaps you could save them single-handedly,' she suggested. 'Anyway, apart from anything else, you are lucky to get the opportunity.'

'Don't start that again, Mum. Anyway, I told them they could stuff it.'

'You didn't? Oh for goodness sake, Mel.'

'I didn't say that exactly.' For the first time this morning she smiled, expert at winding Angela up. 'I just said that, after I'd thought about it, it wasn't the kind of job I was looking for and I didn't want to waste their time with a second interview. So we left it at that.'

Would she have got a second interview? Angela sighed but it was done and there was no point in doing a post-mortem. It was the same with every job she applied for and she only bothered to do that because Angela insisted. She usually got an interview, her private education, pleasant speaking voice and smart turnout counting for something, but her complete lack of enthusiasm did the trick every time because the truth was, with the extravagant monthly allowance her father gave her, she did not need a job.

Angela was in favour of adopting a tough love approach; stopping the allowance,

13

kicking her out of the comfortable life she led here and then she would have to get a job and a place of her own and do *something* because the money they had set aside for her, the quarter of a million, was locked away in a trust fund and would not kick in until her twenty-fifth birthday.

It was not asking much for her to fend for herself for the next seven years and it might work because things were getting desperate with her either lounging round the house, out in her brand-new car, bought by her father, or off on one of her infamous shopping sprees, the last being a three-day jaunt to Milan with the obligatory first-class air travel.

'Are there any letters for me? Who's this from?'

It was *the* letter in the pale-blue envelope that Angela had put aside earlier.

'It's not important.' Melanie would never believe it was from her cousin Adele.

'Handwritten?'

'I think it's from somebody at a W.I. wanting me to give a talk. I have been expecting it.' Astonished at the speed with which she came up with lies where Cheryl was concerned, she held out her hand and Melanie with just a passing glance at the letter gave it back.

'Will you do it?'

14

'Do what?'

'The talk of course.'

'Maybe.'

'It's a long way to go.' Melanie could be sharp-eyed for in that passing glance she too had noticed where it came from. 'I bet they won't pay for petrol and a hotel.'

'Don't be daft. Of course they won't.'

'I thought you didn't like doing talks. Why did you agree to do it?'

She was in danger here of getting into very deep water and Melanie was looking at her expectantly. But whilst she always knew when Melanie was telling the truth she hoped that, on this occasion, Melanie would not spot that *she* was lying and it could hardly be termed a white lie either.

'You're right, I don't enjoy them, but people are interested in what I have to say, how the win changed my life and everything. I always make a point of accepting any payment and they're happy that it goes to charity.' Having got that out of the way, she smiled at her daughter and stood up to avoid further discussion about the mythical W.I. talk. 'I'll leave you to finish your coffee. I'm just going to have a stroll round the garden.'

'Are you having lunch today with Barbara?'

'Yes. We're meeting at one.'

'Where are you eating? The Turret?'

'Where else? Do you want to come?'

'I might do that.'

Angela regretted the invitation as soon as she uttered it, but it was done now. Melanie, fair-haired like her dad but with Angela's deep-brown eyes was striking in a sultry fashion. Her look-at-me looks would be more at home in Cannes and there was no way Angela could disappear under the radar with her in tow, not in Camsdale which was more of a large village than a small town. She was proud of her daughter's good looks, of course she was, but she was not proud of the way she behaved towards her and Tom, and ashamed of the cavalier way she treated others. She was brusque towards the staff; Rachel and Audrey who had known Mel since she was a child, more family friends now than employees.

Why couldn't Melanie be more like her cousin Louisa who was a lovely girl both in looks and temperament? Her sister Moira had two daughters, Adele and Louisa who was just a little younger than Melanie. Melanie was every bit as bright as Louisa but it was Louisa, educated at that common or garden comprehensive, who had knuckled down when it mattered to make sure of securing her place at university. She was determined to be a doctor and knowing her, Angela would be surprised if that did not come about. Perhaps she might ask her sister Moira to have a word because they had always been close and Moira was one step removed from the awkward mother/daughter thing. Mind you, Melanie found Moira's occupation so distressing that she never mentioned it.

That was rich coming from somebody who was yet to find an occupation of any kind.

She could place the blame squarely on the exclusive extremely expensive private school but that was unfair for they had done their best with what was available. Melanie would be a rich woman at twenty-five and the worry was that decent men would be put off by the money coming her way and that she would be left with money-grabbers who would care little for her.

Something had to be done and because Tom refused to consider that there was any lasting problem with his darling daughter, it was up to her to take care of it. But, at the moment, just what that might be eluded her.

2

That same morning, on the western edge of the bay, Angela's sister Moira Rayner was sitting in her car in a single track lane engaged in a stand-off with the driver of the car opposite. The final bit of the drive to her mother Dilys's house was a nightmare with stone walls either side of the narrow lane and she had more than enough scratches on her car so she was not risking any more.

She sat there impassively, determined to stand her ground.

No way was she reversing all the way to the road when this man in an enormous muck-laden van could go back just a few yards to a passing place.

It was a question of assertiveness, stubbornness, bloody-mindedness, call it what you will.

Yes! . . . with a wave of his hand — or had it been a rude gesture — he started to back up and Moira waved cheerfully at him mouthing a thank you as she passed by. The road led into the small estate of bungalows and as she pulled the car into the drive the front door opened immediately.

'Sorry I'm late,' Moira said, giving her a hug. 'Terrible traffic.'

It was not true but she felt obliged to offer up an excuse. She tried not to regard these visits as a chore, but sometimes her mum could be so damned rude to her that she felt like throttling her. Because she lived a short drive away, she was the one who did the bulk of the visiting, Angela deigning to appear occasionally and yet it was Angela who was talked of so fondly, Angela who could do no wrong, Angela who had married Tom, the blue-eyed boy, whilst she, according to her mum, was stuck with Jim.

If she ever did throttle her mum then she would plead mitigating circumstances but she doubted that constantly suffering put-downs and being compared unfavourably to her prettier sister would be a good enough reason to get her off. In any case, she loved her mum to bits. They might not resemble each other in looks but she had inherited her mother's fighting spirit and a tendency to speak her mind, which led to trouble of course.

After a few minutes' further interrogation as to why she was late, her mother finally sat down in the lounge and allowed Moira, whom she considered to be extremely ham-fisted, to make a pot of tea.

Whereas once upon a time Dilys Brierley

had been more than happy to have a tea-bag dipped in a mug, tea-making had now become an art to rival any Japanese ceremony: bone-china cups, a silver pot, cream jug and sugar bowl. In the kitchen, described as compact by the estate agent, Moira sloshed the milk into the little jug and, as she returned the carton to the fridge, realized too late that it was leaving a little trail of milk prints on the floor.

'Bugger,' she said, reaching for a cloth.

'What did you say?' Her mother claimed to be a bit deaf but not so that anybody would notice.

'Nothing. Nearly ready.'

'Funny, isn't it, that when you finally get round to getting the thing you've been dreaming about all your life it turns out to be a disappointment.'

'What are you talking about, Mum?'

Moira moved a vase and put the tray down on the coffee table. The room was stuffed to the gills with furniture for Mother had insisted on bringing a lot of her old pieces with her, refusing Angela's offer to buy her new stuff saying that she did not want to feel she was living in a show house. She maintained that you needed to sit on a sofa for at least five years before it felt right.

'This place . . . just look at it, Moira. It has

no soul. It's nice enough, but it doesn't feel like home and I still can't decide where to put your father. He's been in the bedroom, the spare bedroom, the hall and the kitchen but it's not fair to keep him on a kitchen shelf, is it, as if he's a pepper pot?'

'I don't suppose he'd mind, Mum. He always said you could pop him on the compost heap.' She paused, knowing the answer before she asked the question. 'Are you ready to scatter the ashes yet?'

'No. He's staying put.'

They both glanced respectfully at the urn which at the moment was sitting on its own little shelf in the alcove. Dilys liked symmetry and until she died and they could get a matching urn Moira's father's sat there conspicuously alone. On the mantelpiece the old clock from the old house took centre stage, on either side of that two Moorcroft vases, two candlesticks, then two ginger jars.

She sighed, pouring her mother a cup of tea and passing it over. Dilys sniffed it as if was a glass of claret before nodding and taking a sip. 'You make a good cup of tea I'll say that for you.'

Praise indeed.

'It's not the same living here, Moira,' her mother went on, suddenly deflated. 'And whatever you say won't make a scrap of difference. I'm in no mood for it.'

Oh no, it was going to be one of those days, was it? It was eighteen years since Dad died, but she still had what she called her 'bad' days when all she could do was sit and cry all day. It puzzled Moira because, frankly, she wouldn't have said that they had enjoyed a particularly happy marriage. Her mother had been too overbearing and her darling father, bless his heart, had given in to her far too often.

'Honestly, Mum, you've been here over four years now. It's a lovely spot and you have good neighbours. They can't do enough for you.'

'Only because they know I have money. Mrs Jones was quizzing me only the other day about how much exactly I got from Angela and Tom. I didn't tell her and that really got up her nose.'

'I thought you got on well with her?'

'I do. I used to do her mother's hair.' She scrunched up her face as a memory surfaced. 'She came in every Monday morning at ten o'clock for a shampoo and set. Miserable old soul, never once gave a tip. She had terrible hair. There's a limit to what you can do with fine hair. Look at yours. Anyway, I wouldn't tell her how much I got even though I could tell she was itching to know.'

'So long as she didn't ask you for any. You have to be careful, Mum.'

'You needn't worry. Nobody's taking advantage of me.'

Moira nodded, satisfied because she had the same canny streak as her mother in her veins. 'Most people would give an awful lot to live somewhere like this,' she went on. 'Anyway, you chose it yourself so you've only yourself to blame if you can't settle. You should have gone with Tom's parents to live in Italy. He bought them a lovely apartment there and he would have bought you one too.'

'I know he would. I didn't fancy it. I don't like pasta and I don't like being somewhere I can't speak the language. You never know when you're abroad what people are saying behind your back.'

'You don't know for sure here either.' Moira nibbled at a biscuit as if by nibbling it might not count as a treat. She was petite and it was a constant battle watching her weight. She had done every diet imaginable and come to the conclusion that the only way was to eat less and give up the snacks. She blamed her weight gain fairly and squarely on the size of the plates these days, whoppers they were, and she was trying out an idea of her own, using a side plate for her meals but piling it with food so that it seemed as if she had a lot on her plate.

She did have a lot on her plate at the moment what with Louisa's special birthday coming up and all the preparations that would entail.

'Tea tastes better in a china cup.' Dilys put down her cup and eyed her critically. 'How's the diet going?'

'So so. I've lost two pounds already.' She stuffed the last of the biscuit in her mouth, daring her to make a comment.

She had got the short straw when it came to looks and, as her mother was constantly pointing out she had also inherited her father's fine, wispy, dull brown hair. Thank God for hair colour although she had long ago decided that a short brisk style was by far the best option. The last cut had been brutal, the hairdresser in a bad mood because she had just split up with her boyfriend.

'Bloody hell, Moira, what have you done?' was Jim's reaction to both the reddish colour and the style.

'I can guess what people are saying behind my back round here,' Dilys gave her a knowing look. 'We're still the talk of Woodland and they still expect Angela to fork out a big donation for things even though she doesn't live here any more. They forget it's been five years. Some people would have spent it all by now but Angela's always been good with money, like me.'

'Tom would have bought you a place wherever you wanted, even a bungalow in Woodland itself, but I seem to remember you couldn't get away fast enough.'

'That's right. I might have known I wouldn't get any sympathy from you. You can be hard-faced sometimes.' The sudden glare was penetrating and Moira was the first to look away. 'The truth is I thought I fancied something more rural, but I was hasty. I was overwhelmed by the moment,' Dilys said, in the grand tone she sometimes adopted. With a sigh, she reached for her packet of cigarettes and Moira bit back a sharp reprimand because after all her mother was eighty-one. Her father had never smoked but had dropped dead of a heart attack when he was just short of sixty-nine so her mother always had an answer ready for the smoking question.

'We used to come up here when we were courting.'

'Did you?' Moira gave her a fond glance for she had heard it all before.

'It was your dad who always wanted to live out here and I started to believe that I wanted it, too, and when I set eyes on this bungalow

25

I fell in love with it straightaway.'

'I know. And Angela had her chequebook out as soon as you walked in the hall.' Moira said, knowing the story inside-out. 'And the garden was just the right size and you didn't want to change a single thing in the kitchen.'

'I know. I love a nice tight kitchen. It was perfect.' Her mother blew smoke upwards towards the ceiling and the Edwardian glass chandelier. She did not look her age in spite of the smoking which ought to have ravaged her face by now. She was tiny at just five foot and a bit and annoyingly she hadn't put an ounce on in fifty years so she still cut a trim figure. She had her white hair, thick and heavy, cut at the salon she had once owned, cut gorgeously by the gay guy who now ran it and she dressed well delighted that her legs and feet were in fine fettle so that she could continue to wear her beloved high heels. Moira worried that she would come a cropper one day and that's why, if she couldn't come over, she rang every morning just to make sure she was all right. Her mother could not get the hang of texting so it always meant a phone call.

'Your dad liked the way the hill looms over this place,' Dilys said. 'I thought I did too but it gives me claustrophobia now. All I can see out of the kitchen window is that blooming hill. It's pushing at me all the time. What if it suddenly erupted?'

'It's not a volcano, Mum.'

'It might be. Have you ever been to the top of it? It might be dormant for all we know and just biding its time. You don't take me seriously.'

'You're not saying you want to move back to Woodland?'

'Good heavens, no. This will do me whilst I'm here. At my age it could happen any time. Here today, gone tomorrow.' She glanced heavenwards. 'I haven't specified it in my will but I want you to have that chandelier. It would suit your house. Angela's is too modern.'

'Thanks.' Moira said with a rueful smile. She would rather pull off a fingernail than find that thing houseroom.

'You could have had a house, too, if you'd wanted.' Dilys sniffed, harping back to her favourite topic. 'Angela would have bought you one but then that Jim of yours was too proud, wasn't he? Silly man. There's a difference between being proud and being plain daft. You should have got him to see sense.'

'I'm happy enough where I am,' she said and it was true. 'It's unsettling moving house. Look at Angela. I know she has everything she wants but she lost all her friends when she moved and she hasn't made any new ones and I don't know how she puts up with him. Mr Big-Shot himself. Tom always did have big ideas.'

'Shame on you. The truth is you're just jealous, Moira, and it's time you grew out of that. You were jealous when Angela was born and you've never stopped.'

'I was only a baby myself when she was born,' she pointed out. 'So how could I be jealous?'

'You were, take it from me. I was there and I know. You were jealous when she won the money and you were jealous of her getting Tom. Just because you fancied him and she ended up getting him and you had to settle for Jim.'

'Oh for God's sake, Mum.' China or not, Moira slammed her cup down on the tray and reached for her mother's. 'Have you finished?'

'Don't rush me. I like to savour a cup of tea and in a minute I'll have a top up.' She glanced up as Moira picked up her handbag. 'Don't tell me you're going already? You've only just come.'

Defeated, she put her handbag back down. 'You're always slagging Jim off, Mum.' The remark had upset her and she leapt to his defence. 'I'll have you know he thinks the world of his family and he works damned hard for us. We didn't even have a proper holiday last year.'

'Whose fault is that? You could have gone over to Angela's villa on that lake over in Italy. She told me she offered it you and you turned it down.'

'Jim was on a deadline and we couldn't get away,' she said, weary of it now. 'Anyway, we're having a holiday later this year if it kills us and it won't be at Angela's villa either. We can afford to pay for something ourselves.'

Dilys raised her rakishly pencilled in eyebrows. 'I don't know what it is you have against Tom. I won't have anything said about him. He's a good husband to Angela and he's always been very good to me.'

Moira held back because there was no point in going on about the past, what might have been, because it was well known that sisters nicked each other's boyfriends the whole time. Angela had always been her mum's favourite even if she would deny it vehemently. And for some reason she had never taken to Jim and made no secret of it. He bent over backwards to make her like him, giving her a little cuddle when he saw her and taking her side when it came to the cigarettes even though he didn't smoke himself.

'If I'm taken ill Tom says I can go to live with them.'

'Does he now?'

Dilys gave her a triumphant look. 'Not that I would of course. I don't care for that house of theirs . . . it's like a mausoleum and have you seen that kitchen?'

'I have. You need a science degree to work out how to switch on the oven. Angela says it looks brilliant but it's not best designed for cooking.'

'You can say that again. When I was there I fancied a boiled egg for my breakfast but I'd lost interest by the time I got the water to heat up.'

They laughed.

'The truth is, Moira, I'd rather live with you if it came to it although I expect Jim would have something to say about that. So I want it to be known that I want to stay here with a live-in nurse and I want to die here in my own bed.'

'Don't talk like that, Mum,' Moira said, reluctant to imagine her mother old and infirm. She knew she *was* old of course, but somehow she didn't seem it.

Dilys changed the subject abruptly, asking if she knew that Melanie had got a brand new car for her birthday.

'Yes, it's a BMW, Mum. Must have cost a bomb.'

'They spoil that girl rotten and it shows. She never calls me these days, but then I don't suppose I'm good enough for her.'

'That's not true. She's eighteen,' Moira said, not sure why she was defending her niece. 'They have other things on their mind at eighteen than ringing their grandmas. They hardly have time for their mums.'

'Louisa rings me,' she said, and that hit that argument on the head. 'Don't suppose you'll be buying her a car for her eighteenth?'

'Dead right we won't, but then she hasn't passed her test yet. But we are planning a party.'

'Lovely. She's a good girl is Louisa. Am I invited?'

'Of course. Don't say anything though because I'm trying to keep it secret. I'm hoping Adele will manage it but she'll be on a course that week so it's doubtful.'

'When is Adele getting married, or is she just going to carry on living with this boyfriend of hers?'

'It doesn't matter one way or another. She's not planning to have a baby.'

'Neither was I and I ended up with two of you, one after the other. I was in my

31

mid-thirties and I had the salon up and running so it was a bit of a shock I can tell you. We thought it would never happen and we got careless,' Dilys said tartly and inappropriately. 'And I don't suppose you were planning one when you fell pregnant with Adele and had to get married to Jim?'

Moira ignored that for her mother was adept at delivering below the belt remarks. 'I've met Adele's partner and Michael's very nice. She's twenty-six now, Mum, and old enough to do what she wants.'

'What about Angela? Will you be asking her?'

'Why wouldn't I? I might ask if they want to stay over for a couple of nights, but she'll probably want to book into The Queens Head. If they come that is. I expect she'll find an excuse not to.'

'She will not. She's Louisa's godmother as well as her aunty and that means something to her. Don't forget she's giving her that money when she's twenty-five and it will set her up nicely.'

'I know and we're very grateful.'

'You don't always act like you are. Sisters are supposed to get along. Don't tell me you're still jealous of her winning the money.'

'I am not jealous. I was pleased for her. As for us, well, we might not have millions but we're doing very nicely these days.'

And they had done it all themselves, she might have added. It had been a struggle and a bit of a risk but a calculated one and they had bought the first property at just the right time and more importantly sold it on for a nice profit.

'Call that a business? He wants to get a proper job. I've never seen him yet wearing a decent suit.' Dilys smiled as she stared into the distance. 'Tom has some lovely suits but then *he* knows how to wear a suit.'

She let that one ride. 'Jim's a builder, Mum, and a good one. And I help him with the finishing off stuff. You have to dress a house these days before you can hope to sell it or even rent it out.'

'Dress a house?' She frowned at that. 'I don't suppose you can do any worse than that woman who did Angela's place. She was a strange one if ever there was. And even to this day I still shudder when I think about her feet. If you're going to go barefoot at least wash your feet.'

'I never met her.'

'You didn't miss anything.'

'We made a nice profit on the last house and we've just taken on this terraced property,' Moira said, determined now to hammer home the point. 'It's in a right old state but Jim will soon get it sorted out. We're doing very well,' she finished, determined not to stray into talking about the perilous state of the housing market these days and how it might affect them.

'Fancy yourselves as property developers then? You're just playing at it. You need money, proper money. Like Tom. He's building some nice villas in Spain. Now that's what I call a business.'

'He won the lottery, Mum, and it's costing millions. We can't compete with that. Anyway . . . ' She was annoyed now. 'My business is taking off as well.'

'*Your* business!' Dilys laughed and ended up coughing so badly that Moira felt obliged to get up and pat her back. When she was recovered with the aid of a sip of water she carried on, 'I don't know where to put myself at the whist club these days. One daughter a millionaire and the other a cleaner. It doesn't sound right.'

'I'm not just a cleaner, I run an agency. I'm a businesswoman.'

'Moira's Maids? It sounds a bit suspect to me. What did you call it that for? It sounds like one of those back-street massage parlours where a man can get a bit of you know what.'

'Mother!' Sometimes she wished she was not quite so direct. 'I thought it was a good name, catchy, and I like the freedom, the flexibility of having my own business.' Moira was getting desperate as she saw her mother's eyes glazing over. 'We've just got a contract for that new caravan park and that's worth a lot, but then we have a good reputation because my cleaners are fully vetted and trustworthy and insured.'

'You don't need to sell it to *me*, Moira.'

'But I run it. I'm an administrator. I have to do the weekly wages and make sure the accounts are in order and juggle things around when people are off ill so I want you to understand that I'm not *just* a cleaner,' she huffed. 'Not that there's anything wrong with that,' she finished, on her high horse now. 'I like cleaning.'

'You can run a duster over that mantelpiece then,' Dilys said, glancing at it. 'Mrs Wilkinson never does it properly. She just flicks a feather vaguely in that direction. She never lifts things.'

'That's because she's scared stiff of breaking something. You shouldn't have told her how much those vases cost. Where do you keep your dusters?'

'Oh, never mind. I'll do it myself later. So . . . ' — she stubbed out the cigarette — 'you're doing all right then, financially, because you only have to say and I can let

35

you have something. I have a bit put by.'

'Thanks but no thanks. You know what Jim's like. He doesn't like taking money from anybody. We're managing just fine.'

'Why don't you treat yourself to a new car then? That one's seen better days.'

'I'm not interested in a new car. It gets me from A to B and that's all that matters. I never go anywhere anyway. I only come to visit you,' she said pointedly.

'I'll say this for Angela, she knows how to spend money.'

There was no answer to that.

3

Leaving her daughter to her cup of coffee, Angela stepped outside onto the terrace, breathing in the crisp morning air and pulling her cashmere wrap closer. It was quiet outside, the traffic sounds from the road at the front of the house muffled by the bank of shrubs and the high stone wall.

Angela walked down the shallow steps glancing back as always at the house. After all this time she had to pinch herself sometimes to remind herself that this was all hers. It still amazed her and even as they studied the architect's drawings she had never anticipated quite what the finished effect would be. Her idea for a traditional property had been knocked on the head by the smooth-talking young man with the unlikely name Augustus — call me Gus, Angie — and because Tom's eyes had lit up at all the high-tech ideas Gus was putting forward, she had found herself eventually agreeing to this sleek, open-plan, ultra-modern house. Much about it from the triple-glazed window units to the doorknobs, had been imported at great expense but when money was no object you soon lost track of the pennies.

She could see the merits of the design now as it mellowed and merged into its surroundings so maybe her tastes were changing although the huge interior living space took some getting used to. Unfortunately, her mother had chosen to visit for the very first time when Megan happened to be around and had pricked that young lady's ego with one of her famous put-downs. After a quick tour they found themselves back in the cathedral-like expanse of the living area like a trio of actors on stage as the midday sun sparkled through the windows and shone directly on them.

'Are *you* responsible for all this then?' Dilys asked, fixing Megan with one of her famous stares. 'Remind me who are you again?'

'Megan Jeffrey, Mrs Brierley.'

'Mrs or Miss?'

'I'm not sure that's relevant.' Megan was doing her best to remain civil, unaware that Dilys was deliberately trying to stir things up. Uncertain how to proceed, she glanced helplessly at Angela who obligingly smoothed things over.

'Megan is a leading interior designer from London, Mother. She was highly recommended by our architect.'

'I see.' Unimpressed, Dilys took in the spiky-haired young woman who was dressed today in purple from head to foot even down to purple painted toe-nails. Megan preferred to go barefoot as often as possible and Angela had seen the look her mother had given the not very pretty feet. 'And how much did you charge my daughter for this?'

'It's not about money,' Megan said, speaking loudly as if Dilys was deaf and smiling the sort of smile reserved for awkward old ladies, stooping to address her for, even allowing for Dilys's heels, the height difference was huge.

'Isn't it? It was all about money when I was in business.' Dilys looked up at her, smiling sweetly. 'It's all a bit bare, isn't it, and there's no colour to speak of?'

'It does not need colour. Colour is a mere distraction.' Megan said, still smiling to show she was not offended. 'I am a spatial designer, Mrs Brierley, and it's all about not obstructing the space and showing it to its best advantage.'

'Is that so?' Dilys was unconvinced. 'If you want my advice, Megan, you need a few ornaments around to brighten the place up.'

Megan had rallied and accepted the criticism stoically although the very mention of *ornaments* had nearly caused her to faint on the spot.

The enormous off-white sofas in the living area had cost thousands of pounds each and cushions would ruin the look, Megan said, but when her back was turned, Angela whipped down to a local store and bought some. Damn it all, they were the only thing that made sitting down for any length of time bearable. The sofas might be designed by one of the most respected and influential names in the design world but they fell down in one crucial aspect: for someone like Angela, not blessed with long legs, they were uncomfortable as hell.

★   ★   ★

Sitting on the garden bench, Angela shaded her eyes from the sun which was glinting in silvery streaks across the bay. Tom had fancied himself as a sailor but it had taken only a few trips up and down Lake Windermere to realize that a life on the ocean wave, or indeed the calmer waters of the lake, was not for him. There had been one or two other short-lived excursions into things he had long fancied doing; golf and learning to fly a glider also going by the board when he lost interest.

Glancing round to make sure she was unobserved, Angela opened the letter at last, unfolding and smoothing out the paper. A photograph of Richard fell out and she picked it up, smiling.

It was odd but she sometimes felt that, aside from Barbara, Cheryl Fisher was her only friend and yet she had never met the woman. But it was astonishing how much you could learn about someone from correspondence, innermost thoughts that sometimes could not be spoken were much easier to write down. There was nothing off-limits between them. Cheryl was the pen-pal she had always wanted but never had in her girlhood days. She felt comfortable with her, a woman of similar age and had known at once that this was somebody who would understand, somebody she could trust. With her emotions in turmoil following their win, she needed to get her feelings down on paper but it was a while before she told her pen-pal about Tom's indiscretion. Cheryl had been so sympathetic and helpful telling her in turn about the problems she had with the men in *her* life. They had exchanged a good old feminine grumble about men in general and their men in particular.

For a moment, she let the letter lie idly in her lap, anticipating what it might say and wanting to savour it, for Cheryl was a good letter writer and after she had read it she would lock it away in the drawer of her desk with the others. She knew she ought to throw them away, but she liked the idea of keeping them as if they were love letters. Tom had never written a letter of any kind to her, not ever, but then in the early days they had never been apart so there had been no need.

There was nothing wrong, not exactly, with her corresponding with Cheryl but it was something that she needed to keep secret from Tom because if he knew about it he would explode. As she saw it she and Cheryl were simply friends who chose to communicate by that ancient long-lost art of letter writing. To write a letter, in longhand, you had to make an effort and it took an entire afternoon for her to compose her monthly letter to Cheryl. Cheryl always ended her letters with 'love from Cheryl' and three kisses. The first few letters had had an added 'God bless' but when it was established that Angela was not of a religious persuasion that was dropped. Cheryl on the other hand went regularly to church but she needed to do that she said because it gave her strength to cope.

They had established early on in their relationship that the magic of their correspondence would be lost if they were to

42

actually meet or tell anyone about it. Angela could not remember now whether it was she or Cheryl who had initiated that but it didn't matter because they were in agreement.

True to her word, she never talked about Cheryl to anybody and, aside from this morning, there had never been any problem with anyone else getting hold of the letters before she did. Over the years of their correspondence Angela had built up a picture of Cheryl and her life. Her Uncle Charlie was quite a character, mentioned in passing by a plainly embarrassed Cheryl because he was the black sheep of the family, in prison off and on for minor offences and a pain to the rest of them when he was out. There were no pictures of him and Angela understood why but she could tell from the way Cheryl wrote about him that she was fond of the old devil. She was a compassionate soul but that often happened to women who had a lot to cope with.

Peculiarly, she felt sorry for poor Uncle Charlie, which was completely daft, but sometimes she felt she knew Cheryl's family better than her own.

★　★　★

Tom had changed beyond recognition and there were times when she longed for the old days, the more relaxed Tom, the husband she shared a laugh with, the man she had fallen in love with, the man she actually knew and not this workaholic stranger that he had become. Sometimes, ridiculously, she even longed for the days when money was tight.

The truth was he had adjusted much more easily to this life and there was no way he would ever want to go back to how it had been. He could have given up work, of course, but, as he said to the reporters when the news broke, he had no intention of just sitting around twiddling his thumbs for the rest of his life. He had big plans but his wife, he added with a grin, was definitely going to give up her job in the supermarket.

Standing close beside him with his arm around her, wondering what the hell he meant by *plans*, startled by the flashbulbs and fuss, worried about what she was wearing it would have been plain daft to argue with him then although a full-blown row between them would have no doubt thrilled the media. As the champagne corks popped, all she could do was smile. Melanie was still a little girl at nearly thirteen, and she had felt her shaking, alarmed by the shouts, the flashes of the cameras and the frantic faces in front of them.

Why, oh why, had they not opted for the anonymity that had been offered to them? Why had they elected to go public? Because there had been a great deal of pressure to do so, of course, coupled with the realization that it would be difficult to keep it quiet.

Later, in private, she tackled Tom about the job.

Did she have to give it up? She liked her job.

She was shy by nature and working with people had been just what she needed. It had taken time but she made friends and she knew the customers liked her. She was popular with her colleagues, too, and although they were all overjoyed for her — at least on the surface — she realized that it would never be the same. The day after all the publicity hullabaloo she had gone into work feeling obliged to work out her notice although nobody seemed to expect her. They had played 'Congratulations' on the Tannoy system and the customers in the shop at the time, quickly cottoning on, had smiled and applauded.

If she kept the job and pretended it hadn't happened it wouldn't be long before they were whispering behind her back that she was depriving some other girl of a job she really needed. In any case, with the move across the bay already planned it was out of the question to carry on working there. So, she did the decent thing, treated them all to dinner at a posh hotel, slipped them an envelope with a cheque in it and left it at that.

They promised to keep in touch but when she moved it was a lost cause. The fact was she was no longer one of them and, when she visited Moira, she avoided that supermarket because the ensuing fuss was more than she could take. The one time she had revisited the resentment behind the smiles was palpable.

The problem was it was not easy to find new friends amongst the folk round here because she was shy of just popping round to the neighbours, not without a valid reason, and they did not know what to make of her, neither a local nor a proper incomer, unforgiving and appalled at the construction of what many regarded as a monstrosity. There had been complaints, but in the end their proposal was accepted as the lesser of two evils, the worry being that another developer might seize the plot and try to squeeze in three properties. Barbara Delamere, the only woman to actively befriend her, had stuck by her and even though Barbara was regarded as an eccentric she was her only hope.

Angela smoothed down the first page of the letter. Cheryl had easy-to-read handwriting and littered her letters with trivia which hung about amongst the more serious stuff but that was her way of dealing with the situation she was in. It took some getting used to because in one paragraph she would be telling Angela about the wallpaper in the bedroom and the next would be full of the current problems she was having with Richard. Some of the psychological terminology went over Angela's head but Cheryl liked to pepper the pages with it. At the beginning when they were trying to discover what was wrong, when she, his mother, was the only person convinced that something *was* wrong, Cheryl and her then husband Alan had seen specialist after specialist, palmed off, shunted about, until at last the diagnosis was made and the awful prognosis confirmed that it would not get better.

Some people were doomed to have tragedy after tragedy thrust upon them and poor Cheryl was one of those people. She had had more knocks in her life than a third-rate boxer yet she was one of life's fighters. She had refused to accept the poor odds when it first dawned that there was something not quite right about her little boy.

Just as they had defied the odds five years

ago when they scooped the jackpot.

Tom Ross, 43, painter and decorator of Woodland, Cumbria, was the sole winner and came away with a cheque for £7.3 million.

* * *

The June letter was posted off and there would be a reply by the end of the month because that's how it worked. The routine had been established early on and once a routine is established it is hard to change. The letters from Angela or rather the padded envelopes went to Uncle Walter's address where they sat undisturbed on top of his sideboard until they were collected.

Uncle Walter, knocking on seventy-seven now, sometimes queried them but, bribed with an occasional contribution to his electricity or gas bill he seemed to have accepted the explanation, although despite pretending otherwise, it was obvious he knew damned well there was something not quite right but then he had led an *interesting* life himself so who was he to talk. The fictitious Uncle Charlie was based unashamedly on him adding a few embellishments of course as was the way with artistic licence.

It was hard work keeping track of Cheryl's life so that there were no silly mistakes. The woman had been built up, bit by bit, as if she was a character in a book, the reader discovering more and more about her as it went along. Finding a photograph of the imaginary Cheryl had meant rummaging through a lot of old photo albums to find something suitable — a plain, harassed-looking woman was what was needed, nobody too beautiful or too smart. Cheryl had worked in an office before her marriage to the bastard Alan Fisher who had callously walked out on her when they discovered the child had a problem. There was no need for a photograph of Alan because Cheryl said she had torn them all up.

Cheryl's family tree had been compiled with great care and was consulted before each letter so that at least one of the many relatives could be mentioned to make it all the more credible. It was quite comforting for an only child with no living relatives — aside from Uncle Walter who now knowingly or not played an important part in the deception — comforting indeed to have this enormous extended family even if it was fictitious. Cheryl Fisher had two sisters and a brother and they in turn had families so the family tree was spreading out in all directions. One of the sisters was expecting again and would probably have another boy, name not yet decided, birth date set for early September but mileage could be got out of that situation if the birth was late. A photograph of a new baby was ready and waiting to be dispatched.

Angela Ross might be a millionaire but she was a lonely woman with more than enough worries of her own and it sounded as if that husband of hers was cheating on her. It was annoying that a woman like Angela, somebody who stupidly could not come to terms with being rich, should have hit the jackpot. It was not only unfair it was unjust and that was why there was no earthly reason to feel guilty about the correspondence. Tough luck, Angela, if it ever did come out that this was a fraud, more fool her for falling for it and when you were onto a good thing you stuck with it. Sometimes it was hard to believe that the woman accepted all the lies without query but perhaps it was important to her that she had no doubts that she believed absolutely in Cheryl's existence.

For Angela it must be like writing to an agony aunt; pouring out her thoughts and private worries and being calmed and reassured in the process so what harm was there in it and she could easily afford the little money gifts; water drops in the ocean? It was easy to read between the lines. Angela wrote in detail and without inhibition about her problems because it was true that it was often easier to talk to a stranger than a loved one although they no longer thought of each other as a stranger. Melanie, that daughter of hers, the spoilt brat, was going to be one big problem. Writing as Cheryl, the pen flowed with gentle advice, talking woman to woman, mother to mother, so that when Angela read it, she would find comfort in it.

The letters took some careful composition but that was good for the creative soul. They were checked and double-checked, copies kept to refer to later, and so far, in nearly five years, there had only been one serious error slipping through that mercifully had gone unnoticed.

Pen-friends for years and strangers no longer, closely guarding their secret correspondence, they needed each other.

4

There was something about Woodland that Moira loved. It might be the softness of the pale-grey stone of the houses. It might be the gentleness of the surrounding landscape and it might be the constant presence of the silvery bay that could be glimpsed from certain vantage points all over town, or it might be just that she was born here, went to school here, got married here, her children were born here and everything about the place was familiar.

There was a lot to be said for feeling at home.

If Angela had lived in a big town or city then she might well have moved *here* when she won the money for one of the loveliest houses in Woodland had come onto the market then, a snip for Angela at a quarter of a million. But Angela had always had a desire to live on the other shore of the bay and with the prospect of having a brand new house Tom needed little persuading. Their house might not be to Moira's taste but she did envy them the pool. What she would give to be able to have a leisurely swim every morning in the privacy of her own pool and on the few occasions that she and Jim visited the house she had done just that although on the last visit her morning dip was spoilt by Tom deciding to join her.

The 12-metre limestone-lined pool was part of but separate from the main portion of the house. It was no ordinary pool either for Tom had a sound system installed and coloured lights located under the water so the effect at night was magical. Moira would have adored a midnight swim but the idea seemed slightly decadent and Jim's reaction had been predictably lukewarm.

'What for?' he had said, aghast at the prospect. 'I'll be in my bed at midnight, thanks very much.'

'But it would be so lovely and Angie said we were welcome to do it,' she said, thinking how heavenly it would be to look up at the stars, their bodies relaxing in the warmth of the water before snuggling into towelling gowns, finishing off their swim with a glass of wine before retiring to bed.

'Count me out. You know I don't like swimming,' he said and the blurry romantic vision disappeared in an instant.

So, that last day of their visit, she rose early and made her way to the pool delighting in the stillness of it, the water gently rippling as she eased herself into it. She regularly swam at the leisure centre in Woodland on the ladies only evening but this was something else. She was floating on her back, gazing up at the high vaulted ceiling listening to relaxing music when she caught sight of Tom slipping into the pool and swimming towards her.

'Mind if I join you, Sister-in-law?'

He called her that sometimes, in a joking fashion.

She shook her head, feeling instantly bulky in her black M&S swimming costume with its tummy control panel and supposedly flattering wrap styling. As if that wasn't enough her hair was plastered to her head, her face was flushed and make-up free, a big mistake at her age. Tom's appearance never changed, or if it did the change was imperceptible and, as he swam towards her, he looked like the boy she had known and had such an almighty crush on.

'I thought you were Melanie for a moment,' he said. 'But then I remembered that she doesn't get out of bed until ten o'clock at least.'

And Melanie also just happened to be a girly size ten, Moira thought incredulously, so don't give me that one.

'Glad you enjoy the pool,' he went on,

54

ducking down a minute before resurfacing. 'Great, isn't it? Angie thought it was one luxury we could do without but then she doesn't do swimming.'

'I know.'

'Fancy a race? End to end,' he said cheerfully. 'I'll give you a start.'

'No thanks. I'm finished.'

She swam for the steps and clambered out, tugging at her swimsuit and reaching quickly for a big fluffy towel to hide herself in. The pool was hardly Olympic-size but big enough to enjoy a swim. She could probably match him stroke for stroke but she had no intention of doing so.

★ ★ ★

Returning to their room, Jim was still asleep in his striped pyjamas, looking gloriously unkempt and she did not wake him. These sisterly visits were a chore and that was mainly Angela's fault. She still looked as if she was playing a part, apologizing for having staff, unhappy to be looked after by other people but if she felt like that why the hell didn't she just sack the cleaner and the gardener and do the lot herself? Moira did not have much sympathy for her plight.

As for their men, they had always played

the game of 'I can do anything better than you'; it was laughable and childish and maybe it was something to do with their star signs which hinted at clashing personalities. Sadly, from Jim's point of view, he was unable to compete when Tom won the lottery and just because they had argued the previous week — about something so trivial she could not now remember what triggered it off — Jim's stubbornness kicked in and no, he would not allow Tom to buy him a bloody house.

She finished her hair and make-up, satisfied at the improvement, watching as Jim heaved heavily about the bed, arms thrashing, which was the prelude to him waking up. The black swimsuit was soaking in the basin and she rinsed it out, hung it up to dry and, when she returned to the bedroom, Jim had swung his legs out of bed and was in the middle of his most unattractive morning stretch and scratch routine. Head. Underarms. Crotch. It never varied.

She gave him a wifely look which he ignored, concentrating on the task in hand with a blissful look on his face.

'Been for your swim?' he asked.

'Yes.'

'Enjoy it?'

'Lovely, thanks. It beats Woodland's Leisure Centre hands down.'

Had Tom gate-crashed her morning swim deliberately? Had there been an ulterior motive? The fact was Tom had had his chance with her and he had made his choice just as she had made hers. Even so, temptation was best avoided and she resolved to make damned sure that she and Tom were not alone again because she knew in her heart that when push came to shove she might very well let herself down.

* * *

They had a few visitors here at Woodland, on the edge of the Lake District proper as it was and the great expanse of the bay itself was always of interest. The beach — they were urged not to use the term mudflats for that didn't sound half so pretty — stretched for miles. It was a thriving little market town in many ways and acquiring the cleaning contract for the small caravan site on the outskirts really was a big deal. In fact, in Woodland, Moira's Maids pretty much controlled the cleaning set-up.

With her temper still bubbling because visits to Dilys always left her at a simmering point, Moira drove back home, stopping off to see how Jim was getting on. The property he was doing up was in a small terrace which had bucked the general trend with the owners doing up the outside stonework in a variety of pastel colours — the Balamory effect. Moira had decided on a deeper blue than the one adjoining which should colour co-ordinate beautifully.

'How was the old bat?' Jim asked with a grin. He would have kissed her but she recoiled because his overall was grubby, his dark hair turned grey with dust.

'Don't call her that. She was fine. She's keen on coming to the party.' She looked round for somewhere clean to sit, gave up. 'This is in a terrible state, Jim. Has there been a leak over there?'

'And how. The roof's had it.' He tugged at the safety goggles that lay loosely round his neck. 'Bit of a blow that. I should have checked properly but it looked OK from down below.'

'For heaven's sake, Jim.' It was unlike him to miss something like that. He had paid just over the price he had set himself at auction so a new roof would seriously deplete any profit, so it might have to be another rental until things picked up.

'Fancy a cup of coffee, love?' he said quickly. 'I'll get Tony to put the kettle on.'

'No thanks, I had tea with Mum. I'm not going to hang about. Hello Tony.' She smiled as he came through lugging a heavy-looking cardboard carton. 'I just thought I'd pop in as I was passing. Oh by the way, don't say anything to Louisa about the party. I'm trying to keep it secret.'

'Oops. Too late I'm afraid. You should have told me earlier. Anyway, surprise parties are always a disaster. Isn't that so, Tony?'

Tony, burly, head shaven and multi-tattooed, scary but with a good heart, was on his knees busily trying to get the carton opened, hacking at the tape with a Stanley knife. He considered the question, the knife blade pointing at Moira. 'You bet. It was a surprise party that caused my dad to keel over. He had a dodgy heart and it was just too much for him when they all leapt up from behind the curtain and started singing *Happy Birthday to You*.'

'You are joking?' She eyed the pair of them suspiciously. They had known each other since primary school and sometimes still behaved like those naughty little boys, also, alarmingly, they often seemed to read each other's minds. 'Have you really told her, Jim?'

'Yes, sorry. Anyway, she had guessed. It's not every day you're eighteen, is it, and didn't we give Adele a nice party so why wouldn't we give her one?'

'She's a grand lass.' Tony chipped in,

59

having miraculously accomplished his task without cutting off a finger and now delving into the box and retrieving plumbing bits. 'My youngest lad has a bit of a fancy for her. She's a bonny girl no mistake and he likes a girl to have you know what.' He grinned cheerfully, indicating with his hands cupped over his chest what he meant. He could best be termed as having a clueless nature but he was canny enough to realize he might have gone a step too far.

'Careful, Tony.' Jim grinned too. 'You're talking to her mum.'

'I'm only saying my lad doesn't like skinny girls. Me neither. I didn't mean no harm.' For a minute, anxiety tripped over his face as he glanced at Jim for support.

Dear God. Did anything ever really change? Did men in this day and age still look on women as sex objects? Moira decided to give him the benefit of the doubt. She did not want to deflate the hope in his eyes but honest to goodness the idea of Louisa, her bright daughter teaming up with Tony's youngest was ludicrous. She was also annoyed on her daughter's behalf because poor Louisa was incredibly self-conscious. She worried about her weight, the fine hair she had unfortunately inherited, and not least her large breasts.

60

On the positive side, Louisa had her place booked at university to study medicine and she was entirely focused and going places. Moira did not think of herself as a particularly pushy mother but she had always told the girls that they could do *anything* they wanted if they worked hard enough. She was proud of them, one doing a really worthwhile nursing job and the other planning to be a doctor no less. Since she and Jim were both of a squeamish nature she had no idea where those genes had come from.

'Terry's a nice boy,' she told Tony by way of consolation, although it was a white lie because she couldn't actually bring Terry to mind. 'But she's not getting herself involved with anybody just now. She has to put her studies first so she's not going to be side-tracked by having boyfriends.'

'Pity. He's doing all right, my lad. He's training to be an electrician.'

'Is he really? Well done.'

A shadow passed over Tony's face and she wished she had not sounded so patronizing for she had not meant to. After all, as her mother was keen on pointing out, she was only a jumped-up cleaner herself. And being an electrician was a very respectable trade and you had to have a certain something about you otherwise you could snip the wrong wire and kill yourself.

'He can help us out when he's qualified,' Jim said, giving her a look. 'We're always on the look-out for a good sparks.'

'He's saving up and hoping to set himself up in business one day,' Tony said, puffing up with pride, the remark meant for Moira alone. 'He's ambitious and a hard worker and he'll make a good husband to some girl some day.'

'I'm sure he will.' She smiled to ease the tension. 'I'm off. Bye, Tony. Nice to see you again. Tell Jenny I was asking after her.'

'I will.'

She turned her back on Tony and allowed Jim a quick kiss on departure. He was solid, was Jim Rayner, a good guy known and respected in this town, a man you could trust. He could in no way be called handsome but there was something about his lived-in face that jolted a woman's maternal instinct. She always wanted to tidy him up, straighten his tie, soothe and fuss him and she had known the minute she met him that he would always be there for her, whatever happened, and that mattered. Getting pregnant following a night out had been a mistake, granted, but Jim did not hesitate in asking her to marry him and she only hesitated a little while before she said yes.

Jim was reassuringly anything but a new man, the sort of man who asked *her* what he should wear; the sort of man who was a stranger to the kitchen, but that was largely her fault for she had never encouraged it. She liked to cook and regarded the kitchen as her domain and if that was old-fashioned then so be it. Her daughter Adele's partner Michael mucked in with all the household jobs and that was fine, too, so long as Adele was happy with it, which she was.

She loved Jim and he loved her and although the sparks had faded a little over time he was still capable of being incredibly thoughtful at times. She might not have all that Angela had but what she did have was invaluable.

She loved Jim, but she kept it to herself, deep down and well hidden, that she was still a little bit *in* love with Tom.

★ ★ ★

Moira wondered if Tony knew about the money that was heading her daughter's way although it was probably no secret around here because, following the win, the rumours, fuelled by a very excitable Dilys, had flown about like nobody's business.

The fact was Angela had settled some

money on both of Moira's girls to be available when they reached twenty-five-years of age. Jim had not been in favour of either of them having things passed to them on a plate, especially such a large sum, but he had relented in the end because it wasn't fair to deprive their daughters of the opportunity and they were both sensible young women.

Adele had received her money last year and had used it sensibly, able to buy a small house for her and the boyfriend down in the West Country where they both worked. Buying it outright and having no mortgage meant life was a lot rosier for them.

They could have had a quarter of a million and more for themselves for a house if Jim hadn't been so damned stubborn, but the timing had been all wrong and his pride would not allow him to do it.

But to turn down the offer of a quarter of a million pounds . . . that took some serious doing. In the end she was forced to agree with him or allow it to form a wedge between them, but there had been times when she resented it. Jim was right though, and looking at her sister, Moira knew that the old saying was true, for sometimes Angela looked as if she had the worries of the world on her shoulders.

You could buy a new house, cars, designer clothes, jewellery, holidays, even a new improved face, but it was a well known fact that you could not buy happiness.

5

His driver, Ron, was a quiet man and although Tom always enquired politely after his health and that of his wife, it was as far as it went. It irked Tom a little that he didn't seem able to get through to him, not even talking about sport was enough to grab his interest.

At the outset Tom had invited Ron to call him by his first name in an attempt to underline the way he saw their relationship evolving, but that had gone down like a lead balloon and the man's Jeeves-like obsequiousness, whilst a little amusing at first, now verged on embarrassing. The way he rushed to open the passenger door for Tom when, as often as not, he was already halfway out, drew a few stares from people at the motorway services where they usually broke the journey; the way Ron would walk just that important pace behind him, slowing down if Tom slowed down, determined, it seemed, to make absolutely clear that the two of them were not on an equal footing.

One thing was sure: if Tom hadn't lost his licence he would not employ a driver.

Sometimes he ached to get his hands on the steering wheel, particularly when Angela drove him around. She was a good driver, handled her car with a confidence that she did not display in other ways, but he always wanted to be in the driving seat himself. It felt wrong sitting there beside her, biting his tongue sometimes so as not to make negative comments. He had less than a year to go before he could drive again. What would happen to Ron then was something they would have to consider, but, as Ron was past retirement age already, a hefty pay-off should do the trick.

After reading the newspaper from cover to cover Tom had a lot of time to think on the journey down to Preston and once they had joined the M6 he gave up on all attempts at small talk leaving Ron to concentrate on the driving, his mind turning to the present perilous state of his marriage. The last five years, post win, had caused a whirlwind of emotions on both their parts, disbelief, excitement, delight, anxiety, upheaval and they felt they had a duty to keep upbeat about it. In fact, looking back, their feet had not really touched down yet.

After all it was what they had dreamed about, the things they would be able to do if only they had money. Now they had money and had done most of the things they had dreamed of but something was missing. They were growing apart, slowly and inexorably, and he had no idea what to do about it. He thought back to the old days, the pre-win days, and the way they had been. They had their ups and downs like anybody else but they always rallied round, talking and laughing their way out of bad situations and he could never in those days have foreseen a situation where they might separate.

Now he could.

He had made one mistake just prior to the win, a one-off, one-night stand mistake that he very much regretted and which Angela knew about. Afterwards, he had felt a desperate need to confess when he should have kept his mouth shut, for that woman never meant anything to him, not like Angela. She just caught him off-guard and had offered it to him on a plate, desperate for sex, and it would have taken a strong man to refuse. She could not have made it clearer, no strings attached she had said, and although she was nowhere near as beautiful as his wife, there was *something* about her. No excuses. It was lust, nothing more, and when it was over he had been overwhelmed by an awful guilt. He had to go back next day to finish the job, but she was out, leaving a key with the neighbour who had looked at him oddly as if she knew.

He supposed at that point, ironically just before the win, Angela could have kicked him out, but she had forgiven him, sort of, although even now years later he still saw that flicker of doubt in her eyes. The trust had gone and once that was no longer there, it was an uphill battle to keep a marriage going. Buying her flowers and diamonds no longer meant anything.

She looked wonderful these days, stylishly dressed, and to him she was still the beautiful girl he had married, but they had lost something along the way and didn't talk any more. He had suggested plastic surgery only because she had chatted about it and ridiculed it in that roundabout way women talk and he had wondered if that meant she really wanted the go-ahead from him to do it. That had back-fired big time. He tried to make amends by doing some hasty back-tracking but the damage was done and he had caught her anxiously examining her face, her lovely face, in the mirror. If only he could take those words back, tell her that he loved her just the way she was, that he was happy for the pair of them to grow old together, the old cliché that happened to be true.

When was the last time they had cuddled

up on the sofa together watching television? When had they last laughed together? When had they last made love spontaneously? When had it started to become routine and on her part something to be endured? He knew her too well not to know when she was faking things.

They probably needed marriage guidance, a counsellor, but he was reluctant to suggest it. You ought not to have problems when you had all this money. You had no right to complain when you had all this money. You should be bloody grateful because there was no pleasure in having too little.

'You all right back there, Mr Ross?'

Startled, he smiled at the back of Ron's head. He always sat in the back of the car for comfort's sake because quite often he had papers to look through, often incomprehensible stuff that Sean sent relating to ongoing work and future plans — some of Sean's ideas verged on the insane — but this morning he hadn't looked at any.

'Fine, thanks. The traffic's quite light today isn't it?'

'Yes, sir. Do you want to stop off anywhere on the way?'

'No, unless you need to, Ron. I'm happy just to get there as soon as possible.'

'Will we be staying over tonight at the

Travelodge, sir? I've brought an overnight bag.'

'So have I, but I hope not.'

The fact was Sean had sounded worryingly vague on the phone and unless Tom was mistaken he was up to something.

6

The restaurant in The Turret Hotel was Barbara's choice for lunch.

She and her ex-husband used to run this very hotel before he left her, leaving Barbara to cope on her own. After ten years, she sold it and, although money was rarely mentioned, she seemed to be doing all right, living alone in a newly built apartment. From there, everything she needed was within walking distance, although she preferred to drive, leaving her distinctive little yellow car randomly parked wherever she fancied.

The visitors were out in force today enjoying the sunshine, sitting out on the terraces of the cafés lining the shore as if they were in the Med. It only took a bit of sunshine for the café culture to kick in although to Angela the English never looked completely at ease outdoors always with an eye to an escape route in case it rained.

It was only a short walk from their house to town but there was no pavement on the narrow hilly road and it was a risky business single-filing it and clinging to the edge, so they generally took one of the cars. Melanie had driven her in but changed her mind about joining them rather to Angela's relief.

She took a seat in the lounge asking for a coffee to be brought to her. After five years of living here, she was at last accepted, more or less, in the community. Their arrival had caused a stir at first and even though she was asked to join the various ladies' groups it felt as if she was just asked along for curiosity's sake.

She was welcomed cautiously, but she still felt a little on the edge of things. She said nothing to Tom because he would accuse her, probably rightly, of suffering from a mis-guided inferiority complex.

★ ★ ★

Earlier she had read and absorbed the letter from Cheryl. The content of the letters always had a sobering effect on her, but she wasn't going to allow it to spoil lunch. If Cheryl could cope then surely she could although she had found herself touching the photo-graph of Richard that Cheryl had enclosed; such an intelligent face. He was twelve now and a sweet child and it was so sad to think that he would never live a normal life, never be able to form a relationship because he just did not understand emotions. Socially it was a nightmare and when he had been taken to a café and grabbed a stranger's sandwich because he liked the look of it and not his own, it was some considerable time before Cheryl felt able to eat out again. People thought he was just plain naughty when he kicked off and Cheryl had long since given up trying to explain because a surprising number of people had no idea what autism was. If he had an obvious physical disability it would have been easier but he looked as normal as the next boy.

What Angela admired most about Cheryl was the way she focused on the good things in her life, but now and then the truth of her difficult existence shone through and Angela could almost see the tears that must be in her eyes as she wrote about it.

She stirred her coffee suddenly aware that a lone man sitting nearby was glancing her way. Tom scarcely noticed her these days so it was pleasant to catch what was undoubtedly an admiring look. She knew she looked good, but then she tried extra hard for Barbara. Her cream dress was simple as only the most expensive can be and with it she wore camel-coloured accessories in the shape of a broad leather belt, shoes and bag.

Feeling a little flustered, she checked her watch against the clock in the hotel foyer. She could not make the coffee last much longer and she was reluctant to order another. To her dismay she caught the gaze of the man once again and hoped to goodness he didn't think she was interested in him. Pointedly and probably as a complete over-reaction she flashed her left hand at him so that he could not fail to notice the rings on her finger.

There Barbara was at last, spinning out of the revolving door in a flurry of emerald-green silk.

'Darling . . . ' She breezed towards her, whipping off her designer sunglasses *en route* and depositing them in her over-large handbag. 'Am I late? I've had to abandon the car and hope for the best.'

Barbara looked as if she had been poured into her black leather trousers over which she wore the emerald green silk top, her red hair — big, luxuriant hair — tumbling around her shoulders. She was a good size fourteen, possibly sixteen, but she was tall and could carry it off.

They exchanged a kiss on the cheek, Angela assuring her that she had only been waiting a little while. Acutely aware that the man's eyes were still on her — damn him — she followed Barbara into the dining-room where their table was waiting, one that afforded them a lovely view of all that the picturesque little town could offer. The ambience was everything they could wish for; starched tablecloths, sparkling glassware, high backed chairs, the staff well trained to make The Turret dining experience as memorable as could be. Classical music soothed from discreetly placed speakers and there was a murmur of subdued conversation all around. Their appearance did not go unnoticed but then Barbara was not the sort to go anywhere without attracting attention and she was still remembered in this part of the world *and* in this hotel as a person of renown.

The waiter fussed with the chair and Barbara sat down, inspecting the cutlery critically. After weighing the knife in her hand it fortunately met with her approval and she settled back accepting the menu and pretending she could actually read it without the aid of spectacles. She must be well into her fifties although her exact age was a secret. Knowing the menu choices inside out it took only a few moments for them to decide and then they were left in peace.

Barbara smiled, face perfectly made up, red lipstick to the fore. 'Now, before we go any further, has that gorgeous daughter of yours got a job yet?'

'No. She's driving me mad, Barbara. She went for an interview yesterday but decided it wasn't for her. I don't know why she bothered to go.'

'I have the very thing. I have connections, as you well know, and I have it on very good authority via a reliable grapevine that there's a junior management post coming up shortly in a wonderful hotel up near Coniston. They will accept a recommendation from me and it should suit Melanie nicely. She speaks well and she looks good so that's half the battle. She will have to learn the ropes but she'll move up quickly. Are we having wine or are we being good girls?'

'What?' Angela's mind was still on the hotel job. 'Oh, not for me, thanks. Sparkling water will do fine.'

'If you're quite sure. Do you think she would be interested in hotel work?'

'It's very kind of you to think of her but honestly she has no ambition whatsoever,' Angela said. 'And it's not fair for you to recommend her when she will probably let you down. I can't let that happen.'

'Is it really as bad as that?' Barbara sighed. 'What on earth is the matter with her? I've never had children so do tell me to shut up, but may I suggest something?'

'Please do.'

'Voluntary work either here or abroad. It might be the making of her. Either that or cut her off without a penny.'

'Tom won't hear of that,' she said, the excuses piling up. 'And I would worry myself sick if she was too far away. She couldn't survive twenty-four hours in sub-standard accommodation.'

'Yes, she could. You must face up to the truth, darling: Melanie has just gone a little off line, hasn't she? It could be worse; she could be doing drugs or be anorexic. She isn't, is she?'

Angela shook her head. 'She's just naturally slender.'

'You need to get her back on track and sometimes all you need is a short sharp shock. As I've told you my life was sailing along quite happily and then suddenly it all went pear-shaped when that ex of mine walked out on me.'

'Poor you.'

'It had been going on for years, Angela, before he finally plucked up the courage to go off with her. At the time I was horrified and' — she lowered her voice — 'I actually contemplated walking into the bay and not coming back but it was winter and freezing outside so I decided against it. After all, I didn't want to get my new suede boots wet and I couldn't really face being sucked into the mud before I made it to the sea.'

They laughed. 'You would never have done it, Barbara. You love life too much.'

'You're probably right, but looking back, my husband walking out on me was the best thing that ever happened. Facing up to the humiliation and the sympathetic looks was very hard, but the truth was it was fizzling out. It made me reassess my life. With him out of the way I could make the changes I had wanted to make for a while.'

'Our win was a shock,' Angela said thoughtfully, catching Barbara's surprised look for she rarely discussed it. 'People who say it won't make any difference to their lives are talking nonsense. It changed everything for us in an instant.'

'For the better surely?'

She nodded. 'Of course. But Tom works so hard nowadays that we never have time to do the things we said we would do. If we'd won it when we were closer to retirement then it would have been different.'

Barbara raised her eyebrows. 'I know it's naughty of me to mention it, but I would keep a very close eye on those overnights of his. Remember I've been through it myself. Men can't help it; it's in their very nature. Can't you persuade him to just retire gracefully?'

'I doubt it.'

'Wouldn't you like to spend more time in your villa? I know you love it here but Como is warmer.'

She thought of the blue waters of the lake hemmed in by the hills soaring all around making it her favourite of all the Italian lakes. She adored the small cosy villa with the terraced garden that tumbled down to the lakeside road and nothing would please her better than to spend more time there. That had been the long-term plan for they could only consider it when Melanie was no longer a schoolgirl, but now there was nothing to stop them and still Tom hesitated.

'We only managed two weeks there last year,' she said. 'What's the point? It's sad because the rest of the time it's empty unless the family want to use it. Would you like to use it, Barbara? You would be very welcome.'

'No, thank you.' Barbara did not expand on that. 'How are those villas in Spain coming on? Are they ready yet?'

'I'm not sure. Tom doesn't like to talk about it but I think the first two are finished.'

'Really? Where the hell have our starters got to?' She frowned towards a waiter who seemed to get the message for he scurried off. 'Get the starters out quickly — that was always my motto. If people have to wait for a starter it gets their backs up straight off and that will not do. Anyway, I hear on the grapevine . . . '

Angela smiled. Barbara was privy to rather a lot of grapevines.

'I don't want to alarm you but I hear that the buy to let holiday business has stalled. People are nervous about taking that sort of thing on so it might not be so easy to sell them. Of course, you will always get retirees wanting to move to Spain who might be interested, but I doubt they would want to live in such an out-of-the-way area. I looked it up, darling, and it's a long way from the airport and you know how people hate that. Ideally, they want a drive of not more than an hour, far enough so that they are not disturbed by the sound of planes but near enough so that it's not such a great hassle getting there when they are already tired from the flight and the waiting around at airports. Do you see?'

'Tom doesn't seem worried. So far as I know everything's fine. I've told you we don't talk about it.'

'You should. You need to know what's going on. Shouldn't they be trying to sell the first two? Have they started on the others yet? How many are they planning to build? It's all a bit vague for my liking and I don't like the sound of it. Have you ever seen the blessed things?'

Angela glanced round quickly but nobody seemed to be listening even though Barbara had raised her voice. 'No. I have no need to. I've seen photographs of the site. It's in a beautiful spot, right beside the sea with a view of the mountains.'

'So you say. I've never heard of the place.'

'Neither have I. It's going to be a new resort. There are big plans.' She had to put a stop to this. Barbara was just being nosy and it really was none of her business. She supposed, as Tom's wife, she ought to show more interest in the business but it wasn't as if their lives depended on it so she had rather left him to it. It was something that kept him busy and, at forty-eight, he really was too young to retire. He needed something to keep him amused and acting the part of a successful businessman was doing just that although it was also worrying him, which was not supposed to be on the agenda. She knew that Tom had put a lot of money into it, not sure of the exact figure, and maybe it was risky as Barbara was suggesting, but it wasn't as if he was putting all his eggs in one basket.

Charles Grey, their financial agent, had advised against it and so had she for different reasons. Charles had pointed out it was high risk but, as Tom said, if you couldn't take a risk when you had seven million to play with when could you take a risk? She had been against it because she did not trust Sean but she knew that was not a serious business reason.

'I might go into business myself,' she heard herself saying, wondering where on earth that had come from. 'Tom thinks I can't do anything and I'd quite like to prove him wrong.'

'What's stopping you? Why don't you buy a shop?'

'I have no experience for one thing and I have no intention of doing something on impulse. I need to think about it.'

'Oh come on. There are times when you need to be impulsive, Angela. You could open up a tea-room or an ice-cream parlour.' Her eyes shone at the prospect. 'With my expertise I could help you with it if you like.'

She did *not* like and she wished now that she had not mentioned it for Barbara was bullish when she got an idea in her head. If she bought a shop or a tea-room or ice-cream parlour, Barbara would take over; that much was obvious and she would be in the background once again. No, she needed to do something where she was in sole charge. It was something she would have to discuss with Tom.

She didn't want to admit to Barbara that she was bored rotten these days for, aside from continuous pottering in the garden, she did very little. For a full year following the win there had been so much to occupy her, sorting out just where they wanted to live, dealing with the architect and so on, as well as looking at private schools for Melanie. Initially, she had delighted in handing out large cheques to some of her favourite charities, sorting something out for Tom's family and hers although Moira and Jim had been predictably awkward about it. Only after all that was done did she sit in on the financial discussions as to what to do with the remainder of the money.

She listened but switched off after a while, happy to leave the decisions largely to Tom. In the end, fed up with the whole business, bamboozled with talk of stocks and shares and bonds and inclined to just bung the lot under the bed for simplicity's sake, she was left with her own private bank account into which a substantial amount was lodged. Tom in his turn was happy to leave that to her, never querying what she was doing or how much she was spending.

He trusted her and that's why he must never know what was happening to it and by how much it had dwindled.

7

It didn't much matter where you were based these days, not with the Internet and video conferences and so on, but it looked good to have a business base, modern offices and the like. Working on a shoestring from the bedroom at home as his dear sister-in-law chose to do did not have the same ring about it. Having money meant Tom could afford to set Sean up with a classy business address.

Tom recognized that he was a mere figurehead for the company, although he liked to think he was more than just the man providing the cash. He was always consulted about major decisions but he was happy to take Sean's word for it, keeping him on an extremely loose rein. The problem with loose reins was, of course, that they could easily become tangled.

He knew Sean from way back, a guy with entrepreneurial flair who had made good, moving down to Lancashire when he left school, marrying his first wife Tricia and quickly having two sons. He and Angela had been invited to their wedding and after that they kept in touch in a fashion, the ladies ringing each other from time to time, Christmas cards being exchanged and so on.

After he heard about Tom winning the money, Sean was in there like a shot to ask him if he wanted to invest in a golden opportunity. Sean was keen to point out that he was already successful and was looking to invest in a new exciting venture and Tom, knowing how well Sean lived had no reason to disbelieve him. He and Tricia had just split up. Tom did not let that have any influence on business dealings and whether or not Sean was the guilty partner — and he most certainly was — remained a private matter between him and Tricia.

Sean was interested in taking a high stake in the building of six high-class villas in Spain. It was a potential goldmine in what promised to be a brand new resort and they needed to muscle in on the first wave of development. Each villa would have a large terrace and pool and they were going for quality rather than quantity because the site was so large they could easily squeeze ten on it.

The downside was that the location could be better, off the beaten track putting it mildly. Tom worried about the long distance from the airport, imagining people arriving hot and bothered and in a complaining mood by the time they did get there, but Sean, in his infinite wisdom and with his superior knowledge, cast aside any doubts. Once they were here, he insisted, all would be forgiven. This new resort was going to be one for the future. Driving along the dirt track that passed for a road for the last twenty or so miles Tom was not so sure. Added to that the beach was tight and with severe off-shore currents not the best in the world but Sean was persuasive.

It was a dead cert to make them a load of money but time was of the essence and some other bugger would snap it up if they didn't. This was not the time to start having cold feet, Sean said, for never again would this opportunity arise and they had to snatch at it. Sean could not raise enough cash on his own and needed a business partner to plough money into it so that they could, as Sean put it, get the show on the road.

It had led to a few sleepless nights but eventually with Sean continually badgering him he had agreed to it. It was totally against the advice of the financial chap Charles Grey, whom he came to loathe for all his nervous caution because he only had seven *million* to play with, for Christ's sake.

There had been other deals to consider, people desperate to have him help out but better the devil you know and all that. He promptly injected money into Sean's business empire which included other on-going projects, but they had not reckoned on how long it took to get things moving. The red tape tied them up in knots and the language problem proved to be a headache.

There had been a year's delay before they started on the foundations and then a cock up of immense proportions about the water and drainage supply to the site which had halted work for close on nine months. The local planning set-up had to be seen to be believed making even the thorny outfit at home look like the good fairy. There had been a lot of money changing hands, dubious dealings no doubt, but Sean, shifty as ever, waved aside his doubts. Now with only two villas completed they had been forced to leave the building work for the time being because of some contractual disagreement with the builders which produced a Catch-22 situation as potential buyers were, quite rightly, not nibbling until the whole site was complete and all the builders' rubbish removed. As for the brand new road that had been promised to smooth the ride in, that was turning out to be a pipe-dream.

Sean insisted that they had to be patient and it would pick up once it was completed.

Despite this optimism, a nagging doubt persisted in Tom that he had been duped. Angela used to ask about it but after he had consistently palmed her off she no longer did. He wanted to talk to her about it, about how he felt Sean might be a long-term loser, but that would be akin to admitting defeat. He had got himself into this ridiculous mess and it was up to him to get himself out of it. In the past Angela had always looked after the money side of things and it was his turn now.

He had moved Sean from his previous cramped office to this one bang in the middle of the city, bringing in an office-design team to make it look as professional as possible. Sean dabbled in other stuff that Tom was not interested in and employed a few girls including a secretary/receptionist, although judging by the way Sean looked at her Tom would not be the least surprised if he was shagging her. For some obscure reason Sean seemed to be attractive to the ladies.

In Sean's office hung two huge modern paintings by some up and coming artist, paintings bought by Tom. He had been advised by the arty bloke who flogged them to him that these paintings were a statement and a talking point. They still looked like nothing on earth to Tom, something a four year old might aspire to, but once again he had taken somebody's word for it that they were a good investment.

Tom glanced at them now, appalled and puzzled as ever, before returning his attention to what Sean was saying in that monotonous voice of his. He was struggling to understand the gist of it because Sean always talked in circles and the man looked even shiftier than usual. They were roughly the same age but Sean was taller. Even allowing for his large frame, he carried too much weight and was sweating more than usual, pulling out a handkerchief to mop his brow. He was almost bald, perpetually in need of a decent shave and his suits were always ill-fitting. He paid good money for them, but somehow in the process the whole thing went wrong. Having divorced Tricia, he was remarried with a new baby and the sleepless nights were telling on him. He looked rough.

Every middle-aged man who fancies a newer model should look at Sean and he might change his mind.

This business operated in much the same line as his brother-in-law Jim's but on a much bigger scale of course. No piddling about with doing up a single property at a time for him, as Jim did, and taking on the property market overseas had been something that really appealed to Tom's sense of adventure.

After the initial exciting spending spree — the charitable donations, the world cruise, the new house for themselves, the apartment for his parents and the villa for themselves in Italy, the modest bungalow for Dilys, which he almost bought with loose change, the money in the trust funds he set aside for his daughter and his nieces — he finally sat back, drew a breath and contemplated what to do next.

To placate Charles and his calculator which was attached to him like a comfort blanket, Tom had opted to put some of the winnings into safe-as-houses shares, bonds and so on and, as a safety net, he was glad now that he had been persuaded to put a nice chunk of it into a separate account for his wife.

It was amazing how frighteningly quickly money disappeared though and their house had gone way over budget. He had given Gus and Megan a clear run, not wanting to restrict them in any way and they had accordingly not skimped, although as Angela pointed out the eagerly anticipated wait for the door knobs had hardly been worth it when they looked identical to some she had seen in B&Q. To his irritation, Angela still shopped around, comparing prices of things when they had no need to, shaking her head at exorbitant costs and seeming to delight in getting herself a bargain. She just didn't get it, did she?

He stared at the paintings on the wall, knowing she would go completely daft if she knew how much they had cost. He had put quite a bit of money into artwork and there was nothing to date that he really liked, but then that was not the point, was it?

He became aware of a silence and looked at Sean who had stopped talking and was pouring himself a glass of water. 'Want some?'

'No thanks.' Tom looked at him closely, watching as he saw Sean's hand shake as he took a sip, wondering for a moment if it was actually gin or vodka in disguise for Sean had a flushed look about him these days. 'You'll have to watch it. You look bloody unfit.'

'I'm just tired. The baby never sleeps. I'm too old to have a nipper.'

'What did you call him?'

'Henry.' He pulled a face. 'Thought I might get a daughter this time but no such luck. Sophie says she wants another baby, Tom. Can you imagine? I'm up to my eyes in maintenance for my other lads and she wants to land us with another baby. I've told her no way but you know what women are like when they get broody.'

'We only had one child,' he said. 'And that

was Angela's decision. She had such a bad time with Melanie that she said never again.'

'My point exactly. When it comes to babies, the ladies rule the roost.'

They exchanged a wry smile.

'How was Spain?' Tom asked for Sean had recently returned from a flying visit.

'Bloody awful. Can't stand the heat,' he muttered. 'It's mad out there. It's like stepping into an oven when you go outside and I don't think the air-conditioning indoors helps. It's one extreme or the other. And you've got to wear the old suit, shirt and tie and look as if you mean business.'

Tom made no comment. He doubted if Sean could look the part in whatever he chose to wear. He was capable within minutes of reducing a bespoke dinner suit to looking like something cheap and nasty. He couldn't concentrate today, his mind flicking back to Angela and their problems. Were they sticking together for the sake of their daughter? Melanie was so special to them, especially so because it had been such a difficult pregnancy and birth. It had crossed his mind at one point that he might actually lose the both of them, mother *and* baby, so the relief when they came through it was immense. Melanie had been delicate for a while and they had been grateful for Moira's help.

Good woman, Moira, and she had been the Brierley sister whom he first dated back in the dim distant past. He knew her from school. He could not remember Angela from school because she was too far down the pecking order with that three-year-age difference meaning she might as well have been on another planet.

He went out with Moira for a while, but it was when he met Angela that he upped his game, taking her out in that first car of his, that blue Beetle, taking her to Blackpool of all places. He smiled at that memory, thinking that as a young man a trip to Blackpool had seemed the height of sophistication. The car had been a twenty-first birthday present from his grandparents who had thought the world of their only grandson and he still thought of the both of them with fondness and sadness that they were no longer around. The car was not new and a bit temperamental but he had treasured it and was the envy of his mates.

It had been a blustery autumn day when he took Angela to Blackpool and they had risked getting soaked by walking along the lower sea walk. Later, sitting huddled in one of the colonnades on the north shore, cuddled up and warming each other, he had told her for the first time that he loved her. Oh, and he had given her a silver bangle for her birthday

94

as well which had cost him more than he could sensibly afford. She did not say she loved *him*, not at that moment; instead she smiled at him ruefully, to his delight acknowledging that this was going somewhere and wondering like the good sister she was what Moira would say. 'Honestly, Tom, I feel terrible. She thinks the world of you.'

'And I . . . ' He remembered how bright her eyes looked, deep chocolate-brown eyes. 'I think the world of *you*, Angie.'

Moira had, he recalled, taken it badly, but then she was a bit of a hot-head, one of the reasons it would never have worked. He and Moira had not got round to sex, not quite, but he remembered a few romantic moments in the moonlight, a few hot kisses, more than a few fumblings around at that and, yes, it did feel good.

She remembered them too, he was convinced of that, for a blush was never far away when they met and she rarely looked him in the eye. Theirs would have been a more volatile relationship but never boring. Angela was altogether calmer and quieter than her sister and that had greatly appealed to him.

Sitting in Sean's office, noticing the photograph Sean had on his desk of his new wife, he suddenly recalled with a vividness that shook him the way Angela had looked on *their* wedding day.

For better for worse, for richer for poorer . . . you chanted the words and didn't really think properly about them. They were in the richer zone at the moment and it ought to be wonderful but it was not.

'How's it going, Sean? Are we any further forward?'

He shook his thoughts free and broke into the elaborate ducking and diving that was Sean's default manner of speaking. If they didn't get on with it they would indeed be here until midnight for Sean would expect a long lunch break with a light luncheon wine at some restaurant nearby and then he would no doubt want to have dinner this evening. He had no intention of going back to his place, not happy at having to face the usurper Sophie. Bloody hell, he had liked Tricia and the older boys were great.

'Did you manage to speak to the architect?' he asked, watching as Sean, suddenly noticing it, dabbed ineffectually at a stain on his tie. 'The architect,' he repeated testily as Sean was slow to answer.

The architect was proving elusive of late. Although Tom reckoned he was a good judge of character, now he was starting to doubt his judgement. Whenever he rang that architect, everything was always going swimmingly, progressing satisfactorily and so on. The agent, too, was a slippery customer and very confident that they would have no trouble whatsoever selling the villas when the site was finished. What was there not to like about them? Admittedly the beach left a little to be desired, but what would that matter when the sun shone? And they must not forget the single most important fact for potential English buyers was that English money was involved providing the confidence they were seeking.

'Did he turn up for your meeting?'

Sean ditched the attempt to clean up the tie and smiled nervously.

Suddenly it was if a low blow hit him, waist level, and he caught something of Sean's obvious discomfort. 'What the hell's going on? This is dragging on forever. If it's not one thing it's another. What's the hold up this time?'

'Well, here's the thing, Tom. It's a bit of a bummer actually. They've had to pull the plug on it.'

'What are you talking about?'

Sean took another sip of water. His shirt buttons strained over his large stomach and the stain on his tie was probably baby-sick.

'We've run into trouble,' Sean conceded at

last. 'We should have got an English lawyer to read the contract before we signed it. It's so full of holes it's lace.'

'We had an English translation, didn't we?' Tom was perplexed. 'It's all above board. We were given the green light, the planning permission or whatever the hell the equivalent is.' His eyes narrowed as he caught Sean's look. 'Don't tell me we don't have permission.'

'Not exactly.'

'Yes or no.'

'Put like that, no. We don't. The planning set-up is a farce controlled by the mayor and it turns out we've built on agricultural land that must be used for agricultural purposes only. They were all in it. That sodding surveyor's report was a joke and he took a bribe if I'm not mistaken, and the builder is nothing short of a crook. He's buggered off with our money and nobody has any idea where he is. And now some other planning people, higher up the scale, have retracted the original planning permission for what it's worth, impounded the site and we have to demolish them.'

'*Demolish* them? You are joking.'

'Wish I was.'

'What does the architect say? Didn't he check about this agricultural land, for Christ's sake?'

'He says he's not responsible. We won't get anywhere with him. He's washed his hands of us. There was some sort of clause in his agreement and it gets him off the hook.' He grinned suddenly but Tom was too agitated to find it the least amusing.

'Did you read the paperwork before we signed?'

'Did *you*?' Sean glared at him defiantly. 'I read it, yes, but I might have skipped the small print. Who reads small print?'

'Bloody hell, Sean, how much do we stand to lose?'

Or more to the point, how much did Tom stand to lose?

'The lot. In fact it's going to cost us a bomb. We have to pay up front for the demolition and the clearing of the site.' Sean put the glass down on the desk trying another smile, more nervous this time. 'Let's not panic. Admittedly, it's a bit of a blow, but it happens — you win some, you lose some — and we have to rise above it. I've just heard about another site in France that sounds good. And next time, I'll take a magnifying glass to the small print.'

Next time? Just how gullible did this guy think he was?

Tom had been ploughing money like there was no tomorrow into this project, extra money lately, money honed from some of the safer investments and he had done this without telling Angela because he didn't want her to start fretting. He also needed to be in control. Giving Sean money was equivalent to posting it down a drain and although he had been suspicious for a while it was only just beginning to dawn that he had been an easy target, a man with money who didn't really understand this business.

In other words, he had been a fool taken for a ride.

OK, so he had lost a good bit but he still had plenty left and he must not lose his nerve now.

'There's a bit of a cash-flow situation just now, Tom. We could argue it out but do we really want to start going through the Spanish legal system when we might lose a helluva lot more? So we will have to bloody comply and knock them down; we might not lose everything. I can see a way out if you could see your way to bunging me another half-million. That should do it.'

Tom stopped listening and went over to the window. Two storeys up. For two pins, he would open the window and invite Sean to jump. He had pinned his hopes on this project, something that would convince Angela that he could be successful, make even more money. What would he say to her about this fiasco? Probably nothing. There was no point in worrying her.

Not yet anyway.

This man, this slob of a guy, had lost him over a million already and it wasn't finished yet.

'There's a way out?' He turned to face Sean. 'What do you mean?'

'I just need a bit of cash and all our problems will be over. Safe as houses, Tom. I guarantee it.'

Safe as *houses*? That was a laugh and Sean's guarantee wasn't worth a penny.

'You must think I was born yesterday,' he said, the abstract paintings catching his eye again. If that arty guy was right they should have doubled their value by now so at least that was some small consolation. 'Why would I give you any more money, Sean?'

'Let me explain over lunch. I've booked a table.' Sean smiled.

8

Moira booked the function room at The Queen's Head for Louisa's eighteenth birthday party. It was a little out-dated but a pleasant enough three-star hotel in the middle of Market Street and best of all it had a large car-park. This was vital because she didn't want people arriving looking frazzled in their finery because they couldn't find anywhere to park.

Adele could not make it for the actual party and that was a real shame, but Moira understood why and best of all so did Louisa. Adele was working hard and expected on a course that week which it would be possible but inadvisable to avoid. She did though manage to get over the week before to spend some time with her sister and it felt like old times with the two of them bunking and giggling together in Louisa's room.

It was good that her two girls had such a happy sisterly relationship. She and Angela tried hard and even though it often started out well it usually disintegrated with one or the other of them going off in a huff. It had worked better when the girls were small because when they lived so close to each other here in Woodland the visits to each other's houses in those days generally involved picking up their own child, a quick cup of tea and goodbye and thanks. There was not enough time for arguments. Now visits usually meant a long weekend and with too much time on their hands that never augured well for harmony.

Sometimes she wondered if her mother was not right and that she was in fact jealous of her baby sister from the word go. She wished her mother would give her some credit for running her cleaning business for she had been a good businesswoman herself in her day.

Her father had not wanted his wife to work because he had a good job working for the council, a senior clerk in the surveyor's department, and Moira was still capable of filling up when she thought about him for he had been as good a dad as she could have wished for, the parent she went to from choice when she needed cheering up because her mother was always too busy and slightly aloof. She had inherited her father's short and strong build and the hair, of course. He had in turn given his shy genes to Angela, forever content to do anything for a quiet life and certainly never ever going against his wife's wishes. She saw now that Dilys had been the dominant partner in the relationship just as she was in her relationship with Jim — although he didn't know it — but it was the other way round with Angela who gave in every single time to Tom.

By the time Dilys sold off the business she was employing four full-time hairdressers and several trainees. Why then did she dismiss Moira's business whilst she was quick to praise Angela's ability to spend money when all *she* had done was win the lottery? What the hell did she have to do to get her mother's approval and why on earth should it matter so much that she did?

Trying to understand the way her mother's mind worked was a thankless task and, sitting at the desk in her office at home, Moira dragged her mind back to checking through the list of things to do for the party. She was good at organizing and she was confident the party would go without a hitch.

DJ — ticked off. Flowers — ticked off. The buffet — ticked off. Balloons and accessories — ticked off. Cake — ticked off. She was still undecided about what to wear, always a dilemma on these occasions. The dress she had optimistically bought a few weeks ago was still as snug a fit as ever and she might have to buy another. Angela, of course, would, like it or not, stand out in the crowd, clad in some designer effort as would Melanie, although unlike her mother that young lady would be in her element as the centre of attention.

Thinking of Melanie made her pause and frown.

Melanie had been such a sweet little girl and Moira had been expecting to be present at her birth although it did not work out that way. It had been a horrendous experience made worse because Moira was herself pregnant with Louisa at the time. She had already been through a normal relatively easy birth with Adele and hadn't she told Angela that it was a piece of cake? But then she could never have foreseen the problems with Angela's difficult pregnancy followed by Melanie's equally difficult delivery. At the last there was some complication and she had actually feared for her sister's life although she had done her best as the birthing partner in trying to keep her calm but when, with the baby showing signs of distress, the decision was made to take her down to theatre they all breathed a sigh of relief. Tom, on Angela's precise instructions, had been waiting some-where outside and she remembered to this day the concern on his face as they watched Angela being rushed in. What could she do but reassure him that all would be fine?

'I bloody hope so,' he said, tired and anxious as Moira put her arms round him for a much needed hug. 'I'll never forgive myself if anything happens to her, Moira. I don't know what I would do without her.'

She had known then at that precise moment that Tom did indeed love her sister very much and any romantic feelings he might have once had for her were well and truly gone which, as she was pregnant with Jim's child, was just as well.

Angela, scared and in pain was however insistent that she did not want anybody in the theatre with her so all they could do was wait and she had never known the minutes drag so slowly. Why was it taking so long? Had they lost the baby? Or, God forbid, Angela? Moira found herself praying, for it didn't bear thinking about if they were to face a double funeral. Inside her, her own baby tumbled around and she placed a hand protectively there.

'Why is it taking so long?' Tom asked, echoing her thoughts.

'Hey, come on, they do this sort of thing every day,' she said, talking to herself as much as Tom. 'Baby will be out in a few minutes and then we can all relax.'

Thankfully, she was right and Melanie

arrived into the world a few minutes later, small at barely five pounds, whisked immediately away to the special baby unit as the delivery was not entirely straightforward. Angela was entranced by the baby but her 'never again' was sincerely meant and proved to be the case. Moira even though heavily pregnant helped out at the beginning because Tom was back at work — he couldn't afford to take time off — and Angela, still hurting from the Caesarean was useless at dealing with the baby and so the pattern was established with Angela constantly turning to her for advice.

It was a traumatic year for them all, gaining two babies and losing their dad, but for the next thirteen years, despite the menfolk's underlying animosity, it remained a tight family unit. To Melanie she was much more than just Aunty Moira; she was a second mum because, when the girls were small, she and Angela had a childminding arrangement between them that worked very well. Angela had a variety of low-level part-time jobs that brought in that important bit extra. Moira, always that bit more ambitious, worked three afternoons a week as an accounts assistant in those days but, despite the short hours she was a powerful member of the team and even then she had it in mind that one day she would start up her own business.

As she grew older, Melanie often confided in her and, although Moira was careful never to criticize Angela openly, she gently guided Melanie through some difficult moments when the mother/daughter relationship faltered. Angela had always panicked where Melanie was concerned; over-anxious, over-protective and unfortunately over-lax with the discipline. Moira tried in vain to explain that children needed to know where their boundaries were, but Angela seemed unable to understand this and from the beginning she could not or would not say no. Trouble had been brewing when puberty approached and the lottery win just accelerated it because, whilst they were all on a high because of it, it meant a lot of changes that any teenager would find difficult to cope with.

Melanie and Louisa were more like sisters than cousins in the early years, off to the same nursery then school, primary and secondary. Then, after the win, with Tom determined to educate her privately, Melanie was whisked off to that establishment over on the other shore of the bay. Angela had not been convinced of the wisdom of it all but as usual she gave in to what Tom wanted.

'Aunty Moira, I don't want to go to Larch

Hill,' she recalled Melanie saying, excited yet tearful and bewildered by the whole business that, to be honest, had left the whole family in much the same state. 'You should see the uniform. It's brown and yellow and the skirts are pleated. It's horrible. *And* they wear hats.'

'Sounds nice.' She tried to sound bright although she had seen the brochure Angela had shown her and knew it to be true; the uniform was particularly grotesque.

'Why do I have to leave school and why do we have to leave Woodland? I like it here. I don't want to move to Camsdale.'

'Don't be silly. You're going to have a lovely house and as for the school your dad is quite right: it's always better to get the very best education you can afford,' she had told her, believing it at the time.

'But I won't know anybody and they'll all be posh anyway.'

'They'll be very nice and you'll soon get to know them.'

'Why can't Louisa come with me then?'

'Because we're staying here in Woodland, darling, and we don't want her to be a boarder.' And also because the offer to educate her younger daughter privately had never been made but she could scarcely complain when her girls would come into a lot of money in due course. It was Angela and

Tom's money and they could do what they liked with it. If positions were reversed she would have made the offer to educate Melanie, although the situation would never have arisen because she would never have moved her daughter from a school where she was happy.

'Am *I* going to be a boarder?' Melanie's eyes had widened in alarm.

'No, no. You'll be living close by whilst your house is being built so you can go home every day.'

And so it proved. The house, even allowing for the complicated design, was erected quickly and in the meantime Tom and Angela put their old house up for sale and moved across the bay into a rented place near Melanie's new school. Larch Hill, though, for all the expense and exclusivity had not got through to Melanie and she had spent the time there in such a state of misery that, were it not for the fact that Tom refused to consider the idea, Angela might have returned her to school here in Woodland and let her stay with them during the week. Melanie's grades, instead of rocketing, had tumbled and Louisa had overtaken her and succeeded where she had failed.

Louisa was off to university with the promise of an exciting career hers for the taking whilst Melanie was . . .

What *was* she doing?

★   ★   ★

'Mum . . . '

'In here, love.' Moira smiled as her daughter came through. 'Just making sure there's going to be no hitches on the night.'

'There won't be.' Louisa gave her a hug. She was wearing jeans and her camisole top had ridden up to expose her fleshy stomach. It was not a great look and Moira knew better than to comment. 'Mum, I'd like to bring my boyfriend along to meet you and Dad before then. Can I bring him to lunch on Sunday? Is that OK?'

'Of course it's OK.' She glanced quizzically at her daughter who had never before asked to bring a boyfriend home for Sunday lunch. During the last year in the sixth form at school she had focused so much on her studies that she had not fallen into the trap of having a *special* boy. 'When did this happen?'

'I met him properly last month but I've known him for ages. He was in the year above me at school, but he didn't stay on to the sixth form.' Louisa plumped down on the sofa. 'I know it will be difficult for us with me going off to uni but we're hoping to keep

111

things going. He has a car so he says he can come down to see me every weekend.'

'Does he now? It's a long trip.'

'He won't mind.'

Moira felt a tingle of apprehension. Rare in this day and age, Louisa was a little naïve when it came to the opposite sex. She wanted Louisa to be free to concentrate fully on her medical studies down in Nottingham and she knew that having a boyfriend back home, thinking about him, maybe more trips home than she would have made just to see him, was going to make life that bit more complicated. And having a boyfriend visiting every weekend would put the brakes on her getting to know her fellow students. But how do you say this to a young girl who was — from the look of her and why on earth hadn't she noticed before? — in the throes of her first proper romance. Yes, her daughter was aglow. Oh, the delights of that and didn't she just know it? The thrill of being in love for the first time, the joy you felt every time you saw him, the wonder of it all.

They had had the sex talk — Louisa gently stopping her halfway through and saying that she knew *all* about it — and she hoped that Louisa would be careful if she was contemplating doing it. She felt suddenly shy of asking, wondered if Adele might know, deciding that, if they were, she would be very understanding. Jim would have to be kept out of it for he would consider her far too young. Never mind that the two of *them* were having sex at that age with Adele coming along as a result; somehow it was different where his daughter was concerned.

'He's very nice, Mum,' Louisa said quietly, sensing her concern. 'Don't worry. We're just getting to know each other and we're taking it slowly. When it comes to it I'll sort myself out,' she added, turning away but not before Moira noticed the colour flooding into her cheeks.

'Good girl.' Moira nodded her approval at that sensible statement. She wanted to say much more but she was not sure what advice Louisa would listen to and she needed to think about it before she spoke up.

'Oh, and by the way his father works for Dad.'

'Does he?' The apprehension ballooned and she knew what was coming even before Louisa said it.

'He's called Terry Banner,' she said brightly, eyes shining. 'And I know you'll just love him.'

★   ★   ★

113

She spoke to Adele on the phone that evening and to her consternation she laughed.

'She's only eighteen. It's a passing phase,' Adele said, for all the world sounding like a wise old woman. 'She'll get over it and the only way to prolong it is for you to disapprove. Surely you know that, Mum?'

'Of course I know that.'

'Well, what you are worrying about then? Do you remember Jon Evans?'

'Vaguely. But I always knew that wouldn't last. You were far too good for him.'

And I trusted you, she might have added, but didn't because that sounded as if she didn't trust Louisa and she did, but the child was vulnerable, unused to boys and she did not trust a son of Tony's. There were four Banner boys if she remembered correctly, all of them strapping lads. The other three had fathered more than a dozen kids between them, according to the proud grandfather. Worryingly then the family's fertility was obviously off the scale and even if Louisa was careful accidents of that kind happened.

She should not ruin her career before it even started by getting herself saddled with a baby too young and getting married to a man she would never otherwise marry.

Moira knew what she was talking about

114

because she had been there, done that herself.

★ ★ ★

To her surprise Angela accepted the invitation to stay at their house for a couple of nights. They may as well make a nice long weekend of it Moira had suggested, never believing for a minute they would take her up on it.

Now she was regretting it.

There was no problem about space, for Jim had done the loft conversion and the two of them would sleep up there and hand over their bedroom with the en-suite to Angela and Tom. She hoped Melanie would not object to sleeping on the pull-out bed in the office/guest room. The birthday girl would be the luckiest of all and would be staying in her own room and sleeping in her own bed.

All sorted then.

Angela had sounded distant on the phone but then she always did. She had always been a quiet thoughtful person and so it was difficult to gauge what she was thinking and how happy she was these days. She had everything but was that enough? People at the supermarket where she used to work often asked after her and she always replied cheerfully that Angela was fine for what else could she say? Somebody who had won £7.3 million had no right to be unhappy.

Was all well between Angela and Tom?

She knew she talked disparagingly of Tom to her mother but that was because she did not want to let her guard slip and admit what Dilys probably knew anyway: that she had never quite got over him, her first love, and that, yes, she had married Jim very much on the rebound.

9

Angela lay in bed, becoming aware of the morning light and the pitter-patter of rain against the window. She turned over seeking the comfort once more of the softest and best quality pillow ever. The pillow and the just-right mattress were indeed the stuff of dreams, but the dream she was dreaming was in grave danger of slipping away. Beside her, Tom stirred and she moved away closer to the edge. She did not want any morning sex if he had that in mind and a minute later as she felt his hand slide up her leg, she was wide awake. 'No.'

'Oh come on, sweetheart, it's been a long time. We don't need to get up yet. Let's have a cuddle.'

Once upon a time she would not have objected in the least, knowing precisely where cuddles led, but these days, whenever they made love, all she could think about was the other woman, the one he obviously met once or twice a month in Preston. Did they talk about *her* when they had sex? Did Tom compare the two of them?

'I don't know why we still sleep in the same

bed,' he grumbled quietly. 'We never sleep together these days.'

Comically anxious to avoid his still wandering hands, aware she might very well cave in, she was out of bed before she got her balance properly, swaying and steadying herself before she got a grip and padded over to the en-suite. As she switched on the light, she heard his exasperated sigh, the exaggerated way he plumped up his pillow but even though she hesitated, contemplating slipping back in beside him, it was too late: the moment had passed.

★　★　★

After a lovely June, the weather had turned. Sitting indoors, in her plant-filled conservatory, Angela watched the rain as it swept across the lawn. The view across the bay was shut off, shrouded in the rain-cloud and the sticky sands today were no place to be.

She loved this room with its plump, comfortable sofas, cool grey tiles and masses of indoor plants. It led directly onto the terrace, its potted plants soaking and windswept after the heavy overnight rain.

They were ready for the off but they were not expected until later. She felt guilty at the amount of work she was giving her sister by staying there for a couple of nights, not to mention the undoubted purchase of new bed-linen and towels and so on. Melanie was acting like the princess in the Princess and the Pea fairy-tale wanting to take her own pillow and duvet with her because a cheap pillow and duvet would mean not a wink of sleep.

'Are you sure you don't want to take the mattress as well?'

'That's right. Be sarcastic. And she'd better not expect me to sleep on that pull-out bed in the study.'

'You'll sleep wherever Moira puts you and be grateful for it.'

'I don't know why you're making such a thing about it. Aunty Moira won't mind me taking my pillow. She knows what I'm like.'

'She knows what you *used* to be like.'

Melanie's eyes narrowed. 'Meaning what?'

'Oh, forget it.' She was in no mood for an argument and if Melanie really didn't see what she had become then it was all much too late. She loved Melanie, the image of the tiny baby she had once been often conjured up in her head, but sometimes these days she was not sure she *liked* her. Teenagers with their hormones at sixes and sevens were notoriously unpleasant, unhelpful creatures but when you only had the one child you maybe expected too much of them.

Remembering the little scene, she sighed, not looking forward at all to this weekend and what it might turn up. The brothers-in-law did not get on, never had to be honest, and Melanie and Louisa were nowhere near as close as they had once been. One thing was sure, Louisa would not be getting a BMW for *her* birthday.

What with Tom's Jaguar and her top of the range 4x4 and now the BMW, they had come a long way since the Beetle days. That was Tom's first beloved car but when she was pregnant he sold it reluctantly as there wasn't enough room in it. The bog standard estate that replaced it fitted everything in comfortably and was a good work-horse for Tom's business and completely reliable at that, but then the charm of the old Beetle had been its unpredictable nature.

She tried to persuade Tom that buying Melanie a BMW was too much but the car duly arrived, Melanie pretending surprise — shrieking with delight and throwing her arms round Tom — when she had known damned well she was getting it. Had it not arrived Angela had no idea what the repercussions would have been from a girl who ought not to be having toddler tantrums but still was.

Angela almost wished they had come up with an excuse not to attend Louisa's party but it was her niece's birthday and she loved her and at the last she could not do it. Rather to her surprise Melanie had instantly said she was coming too which was a blessing or a curse depending which way you looked at it.

'Ah, there you are.' Tom came through wearing black slim-fitting trousers and a polo-necked sweater. Thankfully he seemed to have forgiven her for the snub he had received first thing. 'What a morning! I was going to have a run but I've put it off until later. It might brighten up before we have to go. I can't believe the change in temperature when the sun goes in.'

She grunted, not in the mood for a meteorological discussion.

'Do you want some lemonade?'

'Thanks. Is Melanie out?'

'She's gone into town for some last minute bits and pieces.' Angela sighed, picking up her own glass. 'I've told her that she's got to be careful not to over-dress but she's insisting on taking that new dress she bought in Paris and *that* handbag and I just know she's going to tell everybody how much they cost. The handbag was two thousand euros, would you believe?'

'Stop worrying. She's a pretty girl and

she'll get away with it.'

'Yes, but it is Louisa's special day and I don't want Melanie to steal her thunder. You know how she loves an audience.'

'Louisa knows how to deal with Melanie. She'll cut her down to size.'

She eyed him closely. 'Is something the matter, Tom?'

He looked up. 'Apart from you not wanting to make love to me any more?'

'Ssh.' She glanced around quickly but they were alone. 'That's not true,' she hissed, feeling herself flushing.

'Isn't it?'

'Don't change the subject.'

'But it's something we have to talk about it, my darling.'

She shook her head. She liked him to call her 'his darling' and for a moment her heart warmed towards him and she wanted so much to run to him and to be held close. Why couldn't she do it? Why on earth did she feel this need to hold back? 'If there's something wrong with the business, I want to know. You seem to be worried sick about something. Please tell me.'

She had been married to him for too long not to be aware of a change of mood, something she had been noticing for weeks now. She wondered just what he was hiding from her, aside from the obvious. The thought that he might be thinking of leaving her was uppermost in her mind. It happened. It had happened to Barbara and to poor Tricia who hadn't known where to put herself when it did, although thankfully she was coping with it now. In fact, it looked as if Sean had come off worse, a bit older than Tom and lumbered with a new baby and a wife who, as Tricia gleefully informed her, wanted several more.

She had thought about the possibility of Tom doing the same thing for some time now and what she would do if it happened. She would not go under, that was for sure, and she would be all right financially. She would cross the bay back to Woodland. Melanie was old enough to make up her own mind which of them she would choose to live with. She was therefore fully prepared if Tom should make the decision to leave her. The way she felt just now the woman was more than welcome to him. In some ways it would be a weight off her mind and probably for the best. She might very well be better off without him.

If you considered something for long enough you almost came to believe it.

★ ★ ★

'Can we talk a minute?'

'That's what we're doing, isn't it?' She bit her lip, wondering why their conversations sounded so stilted these days as if they were strangers, wondered, too, why her replies often sounded guarded and defensive.

'What's happening to us, Angie?'

'What do you mean? We're fine, aren't we?'

'Are we?'

'You're not still on about this morning? A relationship is not all about . . . ' — she lowered her voice — ' . . . sex.'

'But it plays a bloody important part,' he said with a smile. 'I don't like it that you seem to have gone off me.'

'I haven't. That side of life tails off as you get older. It's a well known fact.'

'Who says? I bet my parents are still at it.'

'Tom! How can you say that?'

'There's nothing wrong. They love each other to bits. He's always got his arm round her. They hold hands. They touch a lot. Haven't you noticed?'

'No, I haven't. I didn't say there was anything wrong with it. I just don't think we should talk about them like that. It's their business.'

'I wish I'd never told you about that thing with that woman. I shouldn't have been so honest. I should have kept it to myself. It's all

124

gone downhill since then, hasn't it?'

'*That* woman. She had a name, didn't she?'

'Mrs Parker.'

'*Mrs* Parker? Didn't she have a first name?' She shook her head as she interpreted his expression. 'You can't remember, can you?'

'She was a client and you don't go in for first names.'

She laughed at that. It was so absurd.

'It was a long time ago and it was just sex,' he said with a wry smile. 'It wasn't that great if you must know and it meant nothing.'

'So you keep saying. You decorated her bathroom and found yourself quite by chance in her bedroom. She gave you the come-on and you just couldn't resist. Her husband was working abroad and she was desperate.' She heard her voice catch, realized that it was still raw to her after all these years. 'It was the middle of the afternoon, Tom, for crying out loud. You could have said no.' That old bitterness, never far away, bubbled up. 'Do you take me for a fool? We might look at other people, we might even fancy other people but when we're married we don't do anything about it. Don't your wedding vows mean anything?'

'Please don't say that.' He tried the slightest of smiles. 'Can't you ever forgive me? One little mistake?'

'I'm finding it hard, Tom.'

'It's over five years ago,' he said. 'Pre-win.'

They divided their life neatly into pre and post-win.

'We were happy once upon a time,' he said almost to himself.

'We *were*?' she queried. 'Aren't we now?'

'I'm trying to be. Don't you see, Angie, I'm trying to make it up to you? I'm working hard to be a success for you.'

'For *me*? What do you mean? You are a success.' She waved a hand. 'Look at all this.'

'But that was just luck. We won the money. I want to be a success in my own right. I want you to see that I'm no loser.'

'I never thought that.'

'I don't look at other women now . . . all right, I might look, but you are right because that's as far as it goes. Why should I when I have you?'

'Don't flatter me.' She frowned, determined he would not get round her this time as he usually did. It was time she took a stand whatever the consequences. 'Our life has changed, Tom, and sometimes I wonder if it was for the better.'

'So do I. At least when I was a painter and decorator I knew where I stood.'

'Up a ladder,' she said tartly and they shared the briefest of smiles. 'Oh for heaven's sake, Tom, what is it? Just look at Melanie these days. She has everything she wants but is she happy? Just think of all the boyfriends and the way she treats them.'

'She's young.'

'I was her age when I met you,' she said quickly. 'And if I remember right it became serious pretty damned quick even if there was that trouble with Moira. I felt rotten about that, Tom, but what could I do?'

'She got over it.'

'Did she?'

He looked at her oddly. 'Yes. She's happy with Jim and she has the girls.'

'Why did you have to go into this property business? You should have retired and we should be spending half the year at the villa doing absolutely nothing.'

'How could I retire at forty-three?'

'You made *me* give up my job,' she said. 'For what it was worth I liked it.'

'Oh come on, you know you couldn't carry on with that.'

'But I have nothing to do.' She smiled ruefully knowing that it was a pathetic remark. What on earth was wrong with her? Where was the incentive these days to get off her behind and do something?

'Then find yourself something to do. What about your charity lunches?'

'They're fine but they don't exactly fill my time up and I find those women intimidating.'

'You're every bit as good as they are. I wish you would stop being a little mouse. Stand up to these people and stop being so apologetic about having money. Use your money. If you want something to do, buy a shop.'

'I am *not* a mouse, Tom, and I do stand up to them, but that doesn't mean I like them. I have no real friends any more apart from Barbara. And why does everybody keep telling me to buy a shop? I don't want to buy a shop.' She sighed. 'Can you hear us? This is stupid. If anybody heard this conversation they would think we were completely mad. Having money is supposed to solve everything, isn't it? That's why people keep buying lottery tickets because they have this dream. We are living that dream and here we are, miserable.'

'Look, Angela, I have to tell you something,' he began, looking down and away from her. 'I don't know how to say it because you are right and it is ridiculous.'

She fell silent. She was not going to make it easy. Looking out she saw that a couple of the smaller pots on the terrace had blown over and smashed.

'The thing is there's been a hitch with the

building work in Spain,' he said. 'We're just going to have to accept that it's been a disaster. All ends up. We're going to lose a lot of money and there's no going back. There's no way out.'

'I don't understand.' She turned away from him as a fresh onslaught of rain lashed against the window. 'What happened?'

'Problems galore. Do you want the technical details, or can you just accept that we've been conned. There's no point in blaming Sean entirely.' She turned her head now and saw his face. 'I have to take some of the responsibility too. The truth is we've made a balls-up of it. I didn't read the small print and you are always telling me to do that.'

'Oh.' Relief flooded through her. 'It's just a business problem then?'

'*Just* a business problem? Didn't you hear me? It's a total disaster.'

He had always been hopeless with money, one of the daft endearing things that she loved about him, and pre-win she had never allowed him such a free rein with it. She had accepted and rather liked the fact that she was the one who dealt with household matters. In the old days he had never so much as looked at the bank statements of their joint account. So why should she ever have thought that having money would change him? Seeing his face, a wave of sympathy swept over her, a compulsion to sort this out for him rushing at her.

'Hey, come on, it's not the end of the world. Maybe it didn't work out as you wanted but we have money in other things. You'll just have to put it down to experience, darling.'

She had not called him that in a while, but if he noticed he did not react.

'Sorry, but that's not the end of it. The stocks have tumbled and the shares have halved and I've pulled most of them before it gets any worse.'

'Is that wise? Sounds like you're panicking.'

'Maybe. The truth is I have lost a lot. I've been checking the books and we're down to the last half-million give or take. Actual money I'm talking about, not the investments.'

'Then we are in a pickle, aren't we? Most people would love the chance to be down to their last half-million.' She caught his eye, but he could not raise a smile.

'If I'd had ten million to play with it would have been different.'

Was he seriously saying that seven and a bit million had not been enough?

'Oh, Tom . . . ' Her exasperation had

reached saturation point. Could he not see the funny side of this? 'How can we possibly have spent over six million?'

'Easily. This house, the two villas, your mother's house, the girls' funds, the donations to charity. How many charities did you have on your list?'

'I got it down to fifty,' she said quietly. 'And it had to be a sizeable sum for each or it would have looked mean.'

'I know, I know.' He waved an apologetic hand. 'But you see how it starts to run away with you. And we have horrendous running costs to keep up. What are we going to do?'

'For a start we are not going to panic. It's just a little set-back.' She could feel something stirring along with the knowledge that she was being set a challenge. 'So we don't have as much money as we did but we still have plenty and we have this house and the villa and — '

'I've sold the villa,' he told her bluntly. 'Sorry, I should have mentioned, it but Sean came up with this sure-fire way of recouping some of our losses last month and you know that we've already had offers, cash offers, for the villa so I took one of them up on it. Sean's suicidal. He says if it wasn't for the boys and the new baby he'd slit his throat.'

'We should be so lucky. I told you not to

trust him. He's a snake.' She was trying to take it in, her mood taking a slide as she considered what it meant. 'I can't believe you sold the villa without consulting me first. For goodness sake, didn't you realize how much I loved it?'

'We hardly ever went there.'

'That's not the point. You should have *told* me.'

'Why? When were we last there? I don't know why you're so upset because you never told me that you loved it.'

'You never *asked*. You shouldn't need to ask anyway. You know perfectly well that the minute I saw it I fell in love with it. I've never felt the same way about this house. It's your dream, Tom, and Gus's. You just tossed aside my suggestions, ignored me and went ploughing on. I hate this place. I hate the open plan thing and there's not a single piece of furniture that I really like, apart from the things in here . . . ' She waved a hand at their surroundings. 'It's Megan's house, not mine.'

'*Now* you tell me. After four years, now you tell me. What's wrong with you?' He was fired up now, eyes blazing with anger. 'This place cost close on two bloody million and you have the nerve to say you don't *like* it?'

'Cost, cost. That's all you think about. I didn't want to move. I never wanted to move.'

'You did. It was you who wanted to come over to this side of the bay.'

That was true. 'Maybe I did but you should have persuaded me otherwise. We should have stayed in the old house, done it up . . . ' She was no good at arguing, feeling perilously close to tears. 'I don't belong in a place like this and now you tell me you've sold the villa, the villa that I loved.'

'I'm sorry you feel like that but it was an opportunity too good to miss. I thought we might as well have the money from the villa in the bank although as it turns out Sean's let it slip through his fingers. His fabulous rescue plan did not work.'

'So you've lost that too,' she said, inhaling a sharp breath, her sympathy fast receding. 'You've been throwing money around like confetti, Tom. I ought to have known you wouldn't be able to deal with it. Did you ever stop to think? Charles Grey's on the end of the phone any time to discuss things with him.'

'Cautious Charlie. Grey by name, grey by nature,' he said with a slight smile.

'Why didn't you talk to me then?' She was calming down for it was too late, the villa had gone.

'Because we don't talk any more and when we do we start rowing about money. You

133

always want to know how much things are costing and we don't need to do that now.'

'Don't we? We wouldn't be in this mess if you'd listened to me. You know what I think of Sean.'

'OK. I admit I made a mistake but he seemed to know what he was talking about and you don't know the first thing about the business world.'

'Neither do you.' Her sigh was deep. 'You should have told me before you sold the villa. We shouldn't have secrets,' she said, uncomfortably aware as she said it that she was keeping one from him. 'For heaven's sake, if you'd have listened to Charles in the first place he would have steered you well away from Sean. He's all talk. You only have to look at him to see that.'

'I know. Don't rub it in.'

Sobered, he pushed at his hair as it fell forward, a gesture she knew and used to love. 'What can I say? I've let you down,' he said. 'I'm a loser, Angie, that's all I am. Seven point three million and I mess it up, but I needed to succeed in something. Don't you see that?'

'And didn't you ever realize that you did succeed with the painting and decorating?' she told him. 'It was a damned good business and you were never short of work. You were recommended and people thought highly of you and you know why . . . ' She had to boost his confidence that had taken a battering. 'Because you were good at the job and don't you dare say it was *just* painting and decorating. I was proud of you, Tom. It was a big decision to set up in business on your own, a brave decision and you made it work so please don't do yourself down. You wanted to go into big business and, let's face it, you don't know much about it so somebody was bound to rip you off. If it hadn't been Sean it would have been somebody else. As for Melanie, don't worry about her. You will have to cut her allowance,' she said. 'And that's no bad thing.'

He nodded. 'Cut it a bit anyway although it's lucky that the bulk of her money can't be touched and thank God, too, that we put some into your account. We might have to use that if we have any chance of staying here. We might have to sell up and move on. Can you bear to leave this place?'

'It won't come to that. We haven't a mortgage.'

'No, but we have commitments. For instance do you know how much it costs per month to heat the swimming pool?'

'Not a clue.'

'Not to mention the cost of the under-floor

heating. We're practically keeping the national grid going.'

'We can turn the thermostat down.'

They managed a rueful smile at that.

'And then there are people who depend on us,' Tom said, determined to spell it out. 'There's the gardener and the cleaner, not to mention what you spend on your flowers.'

'Leave my flowers out of it,' she said sharply.

She was stung by that but then men did not understand about flowers. It was the one luxury she truly adored, the weekly supply of flowers throughout the house brought and artfully arranged by a local florist who, in turn, adored her for she helped keep that little business going. Of all the things that having money had brought her, she rated the plentiful supply of beautiful flowers as the one thing she would miss if it were taken away.

'And there's Ron of course. And Annie . . .'

'Audrey. You always get her name wrong. She's been with us for years, Tom. Long before Ron.'

'What does she do for us?'

'She looks after us,' Angela said, bewildered for a moment as to what exactly they paid Audrey for doing. 'She does the grocery shopping and helps me plan the meals.'

'And we pay her for that?'

'We don't pay her much. Remember she used to look after Melanie when she was younger and even now she cleans up after her . . . ' She stopped, for that sounded awful but it was true. A widow in her late fifties, Audrey had been on their books since shortly after the win, long before she met and married her Ron who came into the equation just at the right time when Tom lost his driving licence. She kept Audrey on the books because of Ron and because she didn't like to terminate her employment because, after all she had done for them, that didn't seem fair. It was the same with Rachel. She was not a particularly good cleaner, as Moira was keen to point out, but she relied on Angela.

'We have commitments,' Tom reiterated. 'We have people who are relying on us.'

To the tune of about £90,000 a year, she thought doing a quick mental tot-up; staff of four Audrey, Ron, Rachel and Malcolm. They none of them earned a fortune but it added up and, horror of horrors, the monthly flower bill was extravagance gone mad, not to mention the money she was sending to Cheryl. She was no longer in control of the budget and now that felt dangerous.

'I hate to say it but we might have to tighten our belts,' Tom finished.

'Let's look on it as a challenge,' she said, beginning to realize this was just what she needed, almost relishing the task that lay ahead. 'We must make a list.'

'You and your lists. You think everything can be solved by a list.'

'It usually can.'

'You're right.' He suddenly took on a positive air. 'Let's lighten up. I assume you still have a nice lump left in your account?' His smile was relieved. 'I know you read *your* statements even if I don't read mine. How much have you got left?'

'Oh, there's Melanie back. Don't say anything to her yet.' She saw her daughter drawing the white BMW to a halt outside. 'I'll make us a light lunch.'

She hoped it did not dawn on him that she had skilfully avoided answering his question.

10

There had been a reply from Angela to the June letter, three and a bit pages enclosed in the padded envelope containing the usual package. On Cheryl's or Richard's birthday — circled on the kitchen calendar so they would not be forgotten — there would be a birthday card and a little extra.

If something was worth doing it was worth going that extra mile and there had been a few abortive attempts before striking gold. Lottery winners get begging letters; everybody knows that, so you must do your best to make your offering stand out in some way.

The pale-blue writing paper was chosen because it had been proved that if you put a heap of envelopes in front of the average person and invite them to pick one out, they will go for the coloured one. Added to that, the writing was very neat so that it was easy to read, for a typed letter was an absolute no-no. You must aim for the personal touch and you must get to the point of why you want some money pretty damned quick before they lose interest and toss your letter in the bin with the rest of the no-hopers.

Even so, most of the earlier attempts must have gone the way of all the rest; into the bin.

The Ross win had come about at a traumatic time when a long-term relationship was finally coming to its inevitable end. Good riddance to *him*. The best that could be said for the split was that it meant a new start in a new place. Thank God for the nest-egg built up over the years, together with the disgruntled goodbye cheque and an even more disgruntled promise of a regular monthly one thereafter so that the bijou flat in an up and coming area of town was just about affordable.

The please-help letters sent off to lottery winners had provided a secret source of amusement for some time, kept secret from Stephen because he would have been mortified. They had no need to beg for money and Stephen, a barrister, would have been not only horrified but also very angry if he knew they were being sent, as he was when he discovered a pile of abandoned scratch cards in the bin.

'What the hell do you buy these things for?' he had asked, flinging them down on the table as if they were an exhibit in court.

'It's my money. I work and I can do what I want with it.' The reply was childish and petulant maybe but a sure sign that their relationship was in its death throes. So, with their relationship over, it mattered no longer what the hell Stephen thought and as soon as the photograph of the latest lucky lottery winners appeared in the paper it sent a little tingle down the spine. Did people who send begging letters ever really honestly think they would be answered? No way. It was just a bit of fun, a bit of play-acting, a lesson in creative writing because it was not easy to come over as heart-warming without being mawkish. That first letter had been nothing short of a masterpiece though frankly it was a shock when Angela took the bait.

Looking at the picture of Angela and Tom as they celebrated their win, there was something vulnerable about the woman, a suspicion that here was somebody asking to be taken advantage of. She seemed a little overwhelmed as she stood there with her husband's arm around her shoulder letting him do the talking although, when pressed for an answer, she did say in a quiet voice that she was thrilled. She did not look thrilled, scared rather and shy. She also looked as if she was sympathetic, a woman who might be taken in by a sob story.

It was worth a try.

In the other attempts, carefully composed letters to previous winners, there was always a child with a life-threatening illness needing money for an operation in the States but those letters had failed to impress and would have failed anyway because that sort of statement could be checked on and it was old hat anyway. There were far too many sob stories of that nature, kids needing urgent medical treatment to save their lives so it had to be something else, something more believable but equally touching and it was then, meeting up accidentally with a neighbour, Paula, a woman who clearly wanted to be friends, a woman with an autistic child, that it clicked.

Cheryl Fisher was born.

Autism was not easily understood, thank God, but devastating for all those concerned and Paula's tale combined with a bit of private research into the problem — a load of books from the library — was all that was needed.

As soon as the reply arrived in which Angela admitted that her husband did not know that she was replying to this, that it might be best if he did *not* know, it was all systems go.

The two of them had a secret.

In the reply posted off immediately so as to keep up the momentum of Angela's interest, the promise was made via Cheryl — guide's honour — that she would never tell a soul, that she would address the letters to Angela herself and that Angela could rely on her absolutely. There had then been a worryingly long gap, a couple of months, when it was essential to be patient and in the meantime make a visit to Uncle Walter to prepare him for yet more letters arriving.

'What's in it for me?'

He was a wise old devil but he had obliged and telephoned when the first letter arrived and afterwards he had to be put in the picture — a little anyway.

'Hang on. What's all this about? What are you playing at? You're telling me I'm going to get more letters coming here addressed to this Cheryl woman? Who is she? And what's she hiding that she has to get her letters sent here?'

'It's just a game we're playing. I need a postal address for her, Uncle Walt. It's all above board.'

He huffed at that, baring his yellow teeth. 'Use a box number.'

'No, it has to be a real address. A box number would look funny.'

'Oh I see. You're up to your tricks again? What's it about this time?'

'It's best you don't know.'

'Why? Am I likely to be stretched on the

rack? It's not a matter of national importance, is it? You're not going to tell me that you're in the secret service?' He laughed his croaky hoarse laugh, but there was no trace of humour in his eyes, cold and grey as a winter's sky. He was not a likeable man, never had been and never would be and rumours had abounded in the family that he had got away with murder. His wife Alma, a grim woman, had disappeared years ago and nobody knew where she was although Uncle Walt reckoned she had buggered off to Australia. He had been totally unconcerned and nobody had reported her missing. It was kept within the family although nobody went into his backyard with its paved slabs if they could help it. 'Why has it to be kept secret? If it was all above board there would be no need for secrecy.'

'It's complicated. I'll treat you when the letters come if you don't say anything to anybody.'

'Enough said.' Uncle Walter touched the side of his nose. 'Chip off the old block, eh? Your dad was a right so and so I might tell you. He wouldn't tell you if you were about to tread barefoot in dog shit, not if there wasn't anything in it for him. Selfish sod.'

So it was an anxious wait when it began to look as if Angela had had second thoughts and a huge relief when at last the reply came in a big padded envelope with several neat bundles of twenty-pound notes, each secured with a rubber band. A note enclosed said it was just a little gift to help out with Richard.

After that, it was plain sailing.

It was enjoyable writing about Richard. It was a good use of creative juices to come up with the tales about him although, because of the conversations with Paula who was glad to get all her frustrations off her chest by talking about her son, most of the tales were true if sometimes exaggerated.

It was horrendous some of the stuff that poor woman had to put up with and it only served to reinforce a long held personal belief that children were grossly over-rated creatures. They were not for everybody and not every woman had a maternal streak. It had meant taking a stand with Stephen who was becoming every bit as broody as a woman in an IVF clinic. His determination to become a father was becoming ludicrous. There were so many ways and means of having a child these days without the need to go through personally, cold, clinical means, and some barmy women were even offering their wombs as some sort of temporary lodging. The very thought was cringe-inducing.

Having a kid had to be a joint desire, but

who would have been expected to look after it when Stephen worked all the hours God sends? The part-time job in the florists would have had to go by the board. Stephen would have been glad because he thought it was a poor choice of occupation even though he had no complaints about the lovely arrangements at home. He provided the money and it was enough to keep the both of them but that felt too much like being kept and nobody wanted to be thought of as that.

It was much better living alone and something that you got used to. The freedom was a joy and nowadays, thanks to the regular extra income provided by Angela, it was possible to do up the flat nicely and have lovely things, the latest acquisition being a mint-green American-style freezer; totally unnecessary for a single occupant but lovely to look at. The money Angela sent made that important difference for the little luxuries of life and living with Stephen for all its problems had been a taste of the good life which was hard to let go.

It was a mistake to appear too greedy and never once had the request been made for a larger amount to allow for inflation for that might be counter-productive. The present part-time job in the bookshop was fun and hassle-free, the bookshop run by a man with a private income who cared little about profit and a great deal about coffee and lunch breaks. The shop was rarely open and that meant lots of time to indulge in trying to complete the crime novel begun years before. Stephen had laughed about that, said it was a waste of time, but one publisher had praised the writing saying the characters were believable even if the plot was hopeless so it was sensible to use that God-given skill and simply adapt it to letter writing.

Cheryl and Richard and the whole Fisher family were real people now.

Looking out of the window a group of kids was playing down below, whirling and twirling on their skateboards. One of them fell off and landed in a heap, remaining so still for a moment that it seemed he might have injured himself. Serve him right if he had because all that spinning and jumping and turning seemed pretty pointless. The kid was just winded and struggled to his feet and within minutes was off again.

Thank God that Cheryl's autistic son Richard, the one written about so movingly to Angela, was all in the mind.

If he was real he would have suffered an unfortunate accident long since.

11

Terry Banner was wearing smart trousers and a new shirt, still creased from the packaging, and even though he had not gone the whole hog and worn a suit and tie Moira found she was oddly moved by the effort he *had* gone to. He was, however, one of those men who would always look out of sorts dressed up, his heavy-set body promising to bulk out just as his father's had in middle age. The slightly sheepish smile reminded her of Jim when he was young although it had to be said that Terry was better looking. There was an openness about him that appealed to her and she had him pegged down straight away as a nice, honest boy.

She hoped, as Adele had suggested, that this was just a passing phase in Louisa's life, her first boyfriend whom she would later look back on with fondness and a little regret maybe. That was what happened with your first love.

Louisa would meet someone at medical school and eventually, but not until they were both qualified, she would marry him and become a GP so that it would be easier for her to work part-time and look after the family she wanted. Two doctors, they would easily be able to afford a nanny and a cleaner so that Louisa would not be too stressed by the domestic stuff.

That was what Moira had in mind for her.

With plans like that, there was no place in her daughter's life for a man like Terry Banner.

★　★　★

July was proving to be difficult to read weather-wise; one day lovely and sunny, the next grey and miserable, the temperatures rising and falling with abandon. Today though was very pleasant and she regretted choosing a Sunday roast when a salad would have been more appropriate. She had the windows wide open to let in some air but slaving over a hot stove was not ideal and doing her hair no favours at all. It was frizzing up in direct proportion to how many times she lifted the meat out of the oven to baste it with the delicious juices. She had the meat out, checking it with a skewer, when Jim walked into the kitchen.

'Don't fuss the lad too much,' he said, seeing the tureen dishes sitting on the worktop poised for filling with vegetables.

'He's from a big family and from what Tony says they don't go in for a lot of fuss. It's plates on knees at their house.'

'Is it? Well it's not plates on knees here. We are sitting at the table,' she told him, noticing he was standing there looking perplexed.

'Can I do anything?' he asked.

'You can get out of the kitchen, you useless sod,' she told him, softening the words with a smile.

The beef was a tender cut from the local butcher and despite the heat in the kitchen she had enjoyed every minute eventually producing a delicious meal with a selection of perfectly cooked vegetables, Yorkshire puddings that she had made herself and a big jug of gravy. To follow, apple crumble with a choice of custard or ice cream and if that was all a bit heavy for a summer's day then that was just too bad.

They ate in the dining-room which looked out onto the back garden; an ordinary garden with a tidy lawn, borders with a few roses and, at the bottom, the garden shed. There was open land beyond that and sometimes sheep from the field wandered right over to the fence and peered over. In spring it was a lamb's chorus out there. They had moved here when Adele was young and for years there had been a little slide and a swing which might be resurrected when the grandchildren arrived although that seemed a forlorn hope with Adele not showing any signs of wanting children and Louisa years away from being ready.

Jim had built a patio, pink and grey slabs, where they sometimes had a barbeque but there would be no barbeque when Angela was here. This garden was like a napkin to her beautiful tablecloth and she was not anxious to draw attention to its shortcomings.

The Sunday lunch went down very well and she was pleased to see that Terry enjoyed his food every bit as much as Jim who had greeted him with a grin and a playful slap on the back before launching into a discussion about football which got rid of any awkwardness. She in turn asked after his mother for she knew that being the youngest son Terry was the apple of his mother's eye and he talked of her equally fondly which was a good sign. After the meal, he leapt up immediately to help with the clearing away with Jim, shame-faced, joining in much to Moira's amusement.

'Leave it to us, Mrs Rayner,' Terry said, rolling up his sleeves. 'We'll do the washing up, won't we, Mr Rayner?'

'Jim, please.' Jim, backed into a corner, had no option but to make the best of it and the kitchen door closed behind the two men followed by the ominous sound of clattering plates.

Moira eyed the closed door a little anxiously. She had used the best plates and she didn't want any of them smashed.

'Does Dad know we have a dishwasher?'

'If he doesn't then tough luck.' She smiled at her daughter. 'Terry's been trained well, I'll say that for him.'

'I know. He's trying to impress you. Isn't that sweet? He's so nice, Mum. He opens the door for me, you know. He's got lovely manners.'

'Yes, I noticed.'

Her mind was on other things. Moira looked anxiously around the room frowning a little and trying to see it through Angela's eyes. With the visit looming, she was starting to suffer a severe case of inferiority. Angela's house was something else; it was always perfect, no cleaner than hers of course, but perfect in other ways with its acres of polished wooden floors, special pieces of furniture picked out by that designer woman, and the views from the windows were just superb. How could she compete? Her house was just an ordinary semi on an ordinary estate, an estate that looked better over the years as the gardens matured. They had bought this house brand new and she loved it still.

'Don't worry. It all looks lovely, Mum,' Louisa said, reading her mind. 'I'll give you a hand before they arrive so you have no need to run yourself ragged. And Melanie will love the little products you've put by the bed.'

By products she meant the little sachets of bath-scents, shampoo and soap that Moira had bought from a specialist shop in town and displayed in a little silk-lined box together with the new Egyptian cotton towels. Just a nice touch, Moira thought, worried a little that Adele's old room, now the guest room/office, was nothing like Melanie's colossal bedroom, her suite in fact, at her home.

'I hope she'll like them. She has very expensive tastes these days. What do you think those two are up to?' She glanced towards the kitchen where the door remained firmly closed and from where she could hear deep male laughter. Jim was an affable sort and got along with most people and it looked as if it was already buddy-time between the two of them, which was — worrying.

She needed to talk to Louisa but with the door liable to open any time it was not the right moment to have a mother/daughter discussion about the boyfriend and, in any

153

case, as Adele had said, too much negativity might very well backfire. She would just have to pray that, left to her own devices and once she was settled at university, Louisa would see sense and it would blow over. She could not help notice, however, how pretty her daughter looked, wearing a summery skirt and a top in a gorgeous cornflower-blue colour that flattered her skin tone. Worryingly, the weight she had piled on during the last year was not coming off though and she had to think of a way of gently telling Louisa that it would really be advisable not to gain any more pounds. There was a thin line — ironic but true — between comeliness and obesity.

'Go easy on Melanie next weekend,' she said, turning to the topic uppermost in her mind. 'She's had a tough time with one thing and another.'

'Tough time? You must be joking, Mum. She gets a cracking amount of money every month for doing next to nothing and she texted me to say she wasn't fussed about getting a job.'

'You would be surprised. I know her and that is just bravado. She failed her exams and, although she pretends it doesn't matter, believe me it does. She doesn't seem to be able to find a job yet.'

'She says she doesn't want one.'

'That's daft. Of course she does and she envies you doing so well so just take care not to say too much about your course and your plans because that will make matters worse.'

'I'll try my best, but it's going to be difficult not mentioning it.' Louisa curled her legs up beneath her. 'Do you think she'll bring her car? The BMW?' She smiled, not seeming to mind in the least and knowing perfectly well that there would be no such treat for her.

'No idea. I wouldn't think so. They'll all come in one car. Probably Angela's because they won't be bringing the chauffeur. At least I hope not. God knows where I'll put him if they do.'

'I'd love to have a chauffeur.'

'You have one already,' Moira said tartly. 'You have two in fact: me and your dad.'

'True.' She grimaced. 'I'll have to pass my test next time and I don't mind not having a car. Really I don't. And when I come into the money Aunty Angela gave me . . . ' She sighed. 'It seems a long way away but I'm so grateful for it. It means I don't have to worry about running up a debt at university because I'll be able to pay it off and have loads left over. I'm not going to waste it, Mum.'

'I know you're not. Does Terry know about your trust fund?'

'I haven't said anything,' she said quickly. 'But it's no secret round here that Uncle Tom and Aunty Angela won the money, is it? He did say that he was surprised we still lived here. I think he thought we would live somewhere a bit more fancy.'

'Did he now? And what's wrong with this house?'

'Nothing.' Louisa smiled. 'Don't get upset. He didn't mean anything.'

'We could have had something fancier if we wanted. Angela offered to buy us another house but we decided against it.'

'We? Or Dad?'

'It was a joint decision,' Moira said firmly. 'That was our choice and I stick by it. I don't regret it.'

'Don't you?'

Sometimes, looking at Louisa, Moira thought that her two daughters were both wiser than she was.

'Your father was adamant,' she said with a sigh. 'He didn't want something for nothing and he didn't want to be beholden to your uncle Tom and I couldn't go against his wishes.'

'*Beholden*? What sort of word is that?' Louisa shook her head. 'What century are we living in?'

'I put that badly. I *could* have gone against his wishes, but I decided not to. It was my decision every bit as much as his, but I did persuade him to let Angela give you that money. He wasn't for taking that either but to refuse it was not fair to you and Adele and it would have upset your aunty a lot too.'

'Thanks for that. I'm relying on that money. Why don't they get on? Uncle Tom and Dad?'

'It goes back a long way. They've never got on. It's a personality clash. Your dad always thought Tom was too cocky for words and much too good looking at that. And the worst thing of all was that Tom could do a nice turn at discos. Good mover, charming and handsome. What more could you ask? All the girls were after him.'

Louisa's eyes lit up. 'Including you?'

'Well, I had a bit of a thing for him once upon a time.'

'So Dad was jealous?'

'I suppose so.' She laughed it off. 'But I'm happy enough with your father.'

She did not wish to elaborate. In any case she needed to get into the kitchen to check what the hell was going on in there because it had become ominously quiet. Jim would put everything back in the wrong place and she couldn't have that.

'He's a good lad,' Jim said later, when Louisa and Terry had gone out to the cinema and they could finally put their feet up. They were cuddled together on the sofa, the television was switched on but they were only half watching the documentary. 'She could do a lot worse.'

'And she could do a lot better,' Moira said, shifting slightly so that she was more comfortable. 'Don't encourage him for goodness sake, love.'

'He thinks a lot about her,' Jim told her, obviously having had a cosy man-to-man chat over the dishes.

'He didn't ask for her hand in marriage I hope?'

'No, but I wouldn't say no if he did, although they would have to wait a while.'

'You're not serious? For God's sake, Jim.' The last thing she wanted was for Terry to get his foot in the door here. She thought she had handled it well, friendly but not too friendly, and making sure there was the occasional mention of Louisa's medical studies which she would be taking up soon. Louisa, her bright and breezy girl, needed a man who was her equal and Terry, for all his cheery nature, was nowhere near her in the intellectual stakes. It never worked, that way round. Jim might be *just* a builder as her mum liked to think, but he had a dry wit and was brighter than he sometimes liked to pretend. He was still capable of surprising her sometimes with the stuff he came out with and she knew, if he had applied himself, he could have gone far.

She had Terry down as a bit like Tony, his father, pleasant enough but seriously intellectually challenged, but it had to be admitted that he *was* a hunk and she had caught the glances Louisa shot his way and seen the admiration there.

All she could hope was that it would all pass over without too much heartache.

In the meantime she had a week to go before the party — invitation now extended to Terry, of course — and even though she felt prepared she must be wary of relaxing too much for it was when you were at your most confident that disaster could strike.

12

The week whizzed by as time does when you are busy and Friday came before she knew it. Everything was ready and she even had time to pop out for some fresh flowers because when you went to Angela's it was like stepping into Kew Gardens. The arrangement of predominantly yellow flowers was sitting in a glass vase which she placed on the table in the hall.

Angela would be arriving soon. She had texted to say they were on their way so, barring hold-ups, Moira reckoned they would be pulling up in about fifteen minutes.

She was starting to panic but then she always felt like this when Tom was around. He made her nervous.

'Behave yourself,' she told her husband, popping up to the loft bedroom where they would be sleeping. She had asked him to change his clothes and she was pleased to see he was now looking more presentable. 'I want you to be nice to Tom this weekend.'

'I will be. But the question is, will he be nice to me?'

'Don't dare take him round to that house

you're doing up,' she instructed as Jim deposited his dirty clothes in the laundry basket. 'And don't talk about money.'

'Bloody hell, Moira, anything else out of bounds?' His grin was unrepentant. 'Trust me, love. I shall be the soul of discretion. *He* will want to talk money though so I can't do much about that. He will go on and on about that project of his in Spain so I can't do much about that either.'

'Just try. Don't wind him up.'

She was already on her way out of the room bustling down to the kitchen to check that everything was ready for their meal this evening. She had considered booking a meal at a restaurant, but the party was tomorrow and she thought it more appropriate to eat at home tonight. She was doing a salmon supper followed by fresh strawberries and cream and there were a couple of bottles of a light white wine that she hoped Tom — who had become something of a wine buff — would not turn up his nose at. Simple fare made special by the creamy dill sauce to go with the salmon and the perfection of the carrots, summer greens and buttered new potatoes that she was serving alongside. Her neighbour had an allotment which was overflowing with produce just now so the vegetables were freshly picked.

'They're here, Mum.' Louisa called out,

from her look-out position behind the sheer curtains of the sitting-room. 'There's only a narrow gap but Aunty Angela's squeezing into it. She's doing one of those awful parallel parks.' There was a sharp intake of breath as Moira came through. 'She's done it.'

'I'm not surprised. She's the only one of us who passed her test first time. She's not got many talents but driving is one of them.'

'Mum!' Louisa frowned at her. 'They're all in the one car. A big 4×4. I haven't seen that before. Oh, here comes Melanie . . . Mum, you should see the heels. She looks thin though. Aunty Angela looks nice. She's got these gorgeous wide-legged white trousers and a grey silk top. Her hair's up. Hasn't she got terrific hair?'

'Yes, darling.' Moira hid a sigh.

'And Uncle Tom's all in black. He looks just the same as usual.'

'OK. I've got it, thank you.' Moira dismissed the running commentary, glancing at herself in the hall mirror, tweaking the flowers before opening the door, a big smile of welcome on her face.

★   ★   ★

'There's another one of them little parcels for you,' Uncle Walter said, scratching his

162

stomach through the thin vest top he was wearing. 'This has been going on for years now. Who the hell is this Cheryl Fisher woman? Do you pass them on to her? Am I running a personal postal service? I should be charging her for taking in her post. And why does she use this address anyway? It's a rum business.'

'I've told you, it's complicated.'

It was hopeless trying to answer Uncle Walter's questions and he never remembered what was said anyway. He had been asking the same questions and getting the same answers for the last five years.

They were in the kitchen and, after doing what looked like a week's worth of washing up and wiping down the surfaces it was time for tea which was one of Uncle Walter's favourites: pizza, oven chips and a generous helping of baked beans. Uncle Walter had to be kept sweet and to be fair it was nice to help him out. A memory briefly surfaced of the fine meals enjoyed once upon a time when Stephen was around for he had been a good cook and his way of relaxation after a tough day had been spent in the kitchen.

'Do you want me to slice some bread for you, Uncle Walt?'

'That would be nice. It's not that brown stuff with bits in, is it?'

163

'No, it's white sliced.'

'Good. And I'll have proper butter on it, none of that crap spread. Are you staying? Keeping me company?'

'I'll have something to eat with you, but then I've got to get back. By the way, I won't be along next week. I'm going off on holiday to the Maldives.'

'Where the bloody hell is that?'

'Indian Ocean. It looks lovely in the brochure.'

'You do very nicely considering you don't have much of a job,' he said slyly. 'That bloke you work for can't sell many books, that shop of his is never open so what does he pay you? Not a lot, I shouldn't think. And yet you can afford to go to the Maldives. I bet that's costing a packet.'

'I got the cheapest deal I could and I'm only going for a week.'

'Where do you get your money from? Your dad didn't leave you anything, I know that for a fact. He died owing everybody money.' His smile was twisted. 'Couldn't be doing with you and your fancy ideas, could he? I'm more open-minded myself. Use what assets you've got and you've got the looks if nothing else. So, tell me straight, where do you get the money to go to the Maldives? Is it from that old boyfriend of yours? Barrister, you tell me.

164

Rich bastard then, was he?'

'Never you mind and if you know what's good for you, you won't ask too many questions.'

'You never give me a straight answer, that's why I ask. By the way I've just had a gas bill,' he said, pointing to the sideboard. 'It's there somewhere. Two hundred quid. You couldn't see your way I suppose . . . ?'

The wheedling tone was pathetic, the meaningful pause spot on.

'I've only got a hundred cash on me. But you can have it to be going on with.'

'Thanks.' He pocketed the notes. 'Don't forget the parcel when you go.' He tore a slice off the pizza and scooped up some beans. 'I know you're up to no good and I know when to keep my mouth buttoned, but I'll say this for you. You've got a good heart and you've done more for your old Uncle Walter than that bastard of a dad of yours ever did.'

13

Moira's pale-green patterned sofa from the furniture store in Woodland was a darn sight more comfortable than her own, Angela thought, sitting down with her glass of wine. Moira had excelled with the cooking as usual and they were all pleasantly stuffed. Louisa and Melanie, just slightly reserved with each other at first, had quickly relaxed and Angela was delighted that Melanie had behaved herself. Answering questions about her recent trip to the Mediterranean she had been remarkably subdued in her answers and there was no mention at all of the BMW or the horrendously expensive shopping trip in Cannes.

She had even, unprompted, asked about Louisa's medical course which had caused that young lady and her mother to exchange a look with Louisa playing it down for all she was worth. Angela could not help comparing the cousins and Louisa won in the healthy looks department, plump but pleasantly so with a wonderful peaches-and-cream complexion, her hair a softer shade than Melanie's but then *she* was forever experimenting with the colour.

After the meal, with the tiniest prompt this time, Mel had helped to clear away and Angela, slipping through with the last of the dishes, saw that Melanie was showing off her tattooed ankle to her aunt and cousin. It was meeting with a muted response causing Melanie to adopt a defiant pose.

'Does your dad know about this?' Moira asked, frowning down at it. 'And don't even think it, Louisa.'

'I'm not.' Louisa said with a grimace. 'I don't like them. Sorry, Mel, it's not bad as they go but they are not for me. And Terry hates girls to have a tattoo. He's a bit last century in some ways. He thinks we should be like his mum who's spent all her time bringing up four boys and done little else.'

'Then why is he going out with you?' Melanie asked bluntly. 'A would-be doctor?'

It was a good point. Louisa flushed and there was a moment's silence with Angela and Moira suddenly extremely busy by the sink.

'He sounds great anyway. I like a macho man. I'm dying to meet him.' Melanie dropped the hem of the floral maxi dress, a dazzling mix of hot summer shades, red, orange and yellow, colours that might have looked better on a brunette. Louisa, who had similar colouring to her cousin, was wearing rose pink, her lipstick matching and together they made a pretty pair with just enough of a family resemblance to be mistaken for sisters.

'You will meet Terry tonight, Mel. He's bringing one of his friends along for you.' Louisa, the awkward moment forgotten, smiled broadly. 'I hope you don't mind. It's just a bit of fun.'

'Don't tell me you've fixed me up with a blind date?' Melanie pretended horror.

'I knew you'd be up for it. Leo's coming to the party tomorrow night so you never know your luck, Mel.'

'You haven't told him I'm loaded, have you? He won't be after my money?' It was said in a light-hearted manner but with that underlying ever-present concern.

'No, he won't. If I know Leo, he'll be . . . '

They lowered their voices to a whisper and a lot of girlish giggling followed.

★   ★   ★

The girls, still giddy with excitement, had gone out to a local hotspot — the *only* local hotspot — with Terry and the blind date and the house was silent without them. Tom, following her instructions, was trying his best to avoid confrontational subjects and had gone with Jim to the nearby pub. Angela

168

crossed her fingers that, away from the warning female looks, the two of them would be able to keep their differences on a slow burner.

At last she and Moira could relax.

'What have you got Louisa for her birthday?' Angela smiled at her sister who, after a lot of fussing around, had sat down on the sofa opposite, clutching her glass and looking a bit hot and bothered from her sterling efforts earlier in the kitchen. It was a question she had not meant to ask, but it seemed silly not to.

'Ear-rings.' Moira said. 'Plus a pampering session at the beauty clinic. She's not really into all that but I thought it would be nice for her.'

'Sounds lovely. I don't know how I would cope without my weekly back and shoulder sessions at the salon.'

'Jim does mine,' Moira said, shooting her a look. 'If I feel in the mood, I get the candles out, lower the lights, strip off and he gives me a massage.'

Angela smiled although the sudden vision in her head was startling.

'I read about it in a magazine,' Moira went on, undeterred. 'You're supposed to surprise your husband occasionally and a romantic massage is just the thing to get them going.'

Her sigh was deeply felt. 'It didn't work of course. The first time I tried it he thought there was a power cut when he came into the bedroom and all the candles were lit. 'Bloody hell, Moira', he said, 'don't you know those things are a fire risk?' It took the edge off it, let me tell you. Bless him; he hasn't a romantic bone in his body.'

They laughed and it eased the tension Angela was beginning to feel in *her* shoulders. She relaxed, looking round the room and thinking how nice it was. She ought to have commissioned Moira to do her interior design because she had the knack of being able to strike the middle ground; nowhere near as stiflingly fussy as their mother's house but a great deal more charming than her own. When she got home she was going to make a few changes, she decided, throw out some of that horribly expensive furniture and get something else that *she* liked. She had allowed Megan to take things too far and she should have said at the outset that not one of her ideas was doing it for her. She was just like her dad, far too willing to let people tread all over her just for the sake of a quiet life. Well, finally, she was going to do something about it.

'Doesn't quite compare to yours, does it?' Moira said with a wry smile.

'Don't say that. I like it. I've always liked your house, but then I always liked my old house too. Sometimes I can't believe those people have lived in it for nearly five years now.'

'Do you want to walk past it tomorrow? I should warn you though that they have paved over the front garden to make extra parking space.'

'They haven't?' She sat up straight and the topped-up wine sloshed in the glass.

'Sorry, but they have. I take it that's a no then. You won't want to see it again.'

'No thanks.' She thought of the old stone cottage down by the river that had been their first home and the lovely garden with its little winding cobbled path, the old apple tree and the swing for Melanie. She recalled hot summer days with the little fair-haired girl running around or playing in the little paddling pool, often accompanied by Louisa, and cold winter days when, wearing hats and gloves, they made a snowman. They had bought the cottage for next to nothing because it was falling to bits when they got it and it was a labour of love restoring it to a liveable condition. They had camped out for years in one room and Moira had done a lot of tut-tutting whenever she came round.

'Are you OK, Angie?'

'Not really.' Even as she spoke she felt tears welling up, damped them down at once because the last thing she wanted was to break down in front of Moira.

Moira smiled a little. 'Oh come on, you can't get upset about something that isn't yours any longer. They can do what the hell they like to the garden so you mustn't let it get to you. I wish I hadn't mentioned it now.'

'It's not that.' She bit her lip, her hesitation minimal. 'To be honest, things are not that great between me and Tom just now.'

'Ah.' Moira looked at her closely. 'I thought there was something wrong. I caught you two holding hands when you first came in and that's always a bad sign.'

'Don't joke, Moira.'

'I'm not joking.' Her voice was gentle. 'I know when people are trying too hard. I haven't held hands in public with Jim for ages and we're doing just fine. Do you want to talk about it?'

Angela shifted in her seat, suddenly feeling the need to confess, to open up to somebody and although she might have preferred to talk to Barbara who would take whatever she said on the chin it was Moira who happened to be here and she did look sympathetic.

'I'm not that happy just now and I haven't been happy for ages and I know that sounds

172

mad. Can you remember what Tom said when we won the money?'

'That you were over the moon,' Moira said with a smile. 'I hate that expression.'

'So do I. The thing is, Moira, I never told you this but just before it happened we were having a few problems and I thought that having money would solve everything but it hasn't. They've not gone away.'

'Go on,' Moira encouraged her. 'Don't stop now.'

'There was this woman he was doing some work for.'

'I see.' Moira pulled a face. 'Would I know her?'

'I don't think so. I didn't know her. He did tell me who she was but the name meant nothing.'

'So you're telling me they had a fling? How long did it last?'

'Just the once so he said.'

'And you believed him?'

'I think so.' She ran her finger over the rim of her glass. 'It knocked me for six, Moira. I never thought there was anything wrong between us. How would you feel if Jim told you he had been with another woman?'

'Bloody amazed. He's not exactly Brad Pitt.'

'Please be serious.'

'OK. I'd feel very let down and very upset,' she said.

'Because you love him.'

'Exactly.'

'That's how *I* felt.'

'Why didn't you tell me at the time, Angie? I might have been able to help.'

She sighed. 'I didn't want to admit it was going wrong. I couldn't tell anybody.'

'Did you ever see her?'

'Oh yes. The day after he told me I went over. She lived in one of those Victorian semis on Barrow Road opposite the park. It was a nice day and I sat a while by the children's swings and watched her house.'

'That was daft.' Moira clicked her tongue. 'You would stick out like a sore thumb sitting by the swings if you didn't have a child with you.'

'I never thought of that. I must have been mad. I bought an ice-cream from the van and just sat there waiting for her to come out.'

Moira laughed.

'It was no joke, Moira. And then, suddenly, there she was coming out of her house and I was so incensed that I stood up with my ice-cream half eaten before I realized that I hadn't a clue what I was going to do or say.'

'You felt like thumping her?'

'You bet. It felt like I was back in the

school playground and another little girl had nicked my best friend and left me standing there. Remember that?'

'And how. I used to chase after them and thump both of them,' Moira said with a smile. 'And then I would get into trouble with the teacher and Mum. 'Why can't you be more like Angela', mum used to say, 'she would never dream of hitting another little girl'?'

'I got a good look at her.'

'What was she like?'

'Nothing special,' Angela went on, in her stride now, almost delighting in the telling of the tale. 'Although in a way that made it worse. I could have understood it if she had been this knock-out blonde, but she wasn't. She was ordinary. She was little and plump with short brown hair.'

'A bit like me?' Moira laughed and Angela managed a reluctant smile. 'I take it you chickened out of hitting her, walked home and have never seen her again?'

'Correct. I have no idea if she's still there or if she's moved on. Either way it doesn't matter. I know he hasn't seen her again.'

'It happens.' Moira sighed. 'It could have happened with Jim for all I know but he would have more sense than admit to it. When will people realize that sometimes things are best left unsaid? It's a long time ago and you mustn't let it get to you. I would just forget it and move on.'

'I'm trying to. I did forget it for a while, but I've started to brood about it lately. If he's done it once then he can do it again. Whenever he goes over to Preston for a business meeting he stays over and I keep imagining he's having another affair but this time it's a proper one. Do you think he is?'

'I wouldn't think so. Knowing Tom he would tell you if he was. He's too honest for his own good. He loves you Angela, trust me on that.'

'He did once upon a time, but does he now? We've got a bit of a problem . . . we haven't . . . you know.' She blushed in front of her own sister and couldn't say it.

Moira knew what she was trying to say. 'That's bad,' she said. 'You've got to get that back on track, Angie, or things will only get worse. Is it you or him?'

'Me. I've just got this fictitious woman in my head the whole time. Is he thinking about her or me? I go through the motions now and then just to keep him happy, but I'm sure he knows I'm faking it.'

'Yes, I can see you wouldn't be a very good actress.'

'What am I going to do? Having money

isn't all it's cracked up to be, Moira.'

'I wouldn't mind trying it.'

'I'm sorry. I can't pretend it was great in the old days when we used to be strapped for cash, but somehow I always came through. I had a grip on the money situation, knew exactly how much I had to play with and it was a real achievement when we got through the month without owing anybody a penny. Saving up for things was fun — sort of — making sure Melanie had nice things and all that stuff. Sometimes it was tough but it all balanced out in the end. Tom was a good painter and decorator.' She stopped, took a sip of her drink. 'Sometimes I don't understand myself. It's as if I want to go back to those days and I don't. It's fantastic to have enough money to do whatever you want and I would find it hard buying cheap clothes again. And then there are my flowers, Moira. I love having loads of flowers around the house and I would hate to go back to buying a cheap bunch from the supermarket. Not that those in the hall don't look lovely,' she added.

'Thanks. They're from the florists actually,' Moira said stiffly. 'They cost me twenty pounds.'

'Oh, sorry.'

'Forget it. The thing is you're still in shock, love.'

'After five years?'

'Yes. Why not? It's changed your life and we are never ready for that. We want things to stay the same and they never do. We grow up, we grow older, our kids grow older and there's not a thing we can do about it. Before we know it, Angie, we'll be grandmothers.'

'Thanks for that.' They exchanged a smile. 'Tom's busy doing nothing. He pretends he has this big business thing going on but honestly all he is doing is standing at Sean's shoulder and looking over it. He's let that man get away with murder and all because he doesn't like to admit he hasn't a clue what's going on.'

'Oh come on, I'm not having that. Tom's no fool. He's a bright bloke.'

'I didn't say he was a fool. I would never have married a fool. But he was happier working with his hands. He earned enough to keep us in the way we were accustomed anyway, but now we have the money to keep us in a way we are not accustomed.' She frowned. 'Does that make any sense at all?'

'We all go through bad spells, what couple doesn't? Jim and I have had our moments, believe me. He is the most unromantic man on the planet. He needs to be reminded about my birthday and our anniversary and I can't remember the last time he bought me flowers for no reason. But that's the way he is and I've given up trying to change him.'

'Tom's not much better,' she admitted. 'I remind him about birthdays and anniversaries. He buys me diamonds,' she added with a smile. 'But it's not the same when you don't have to save up for them. They're lovely, of course, but I would love it if he would buy me something that means something.'

'You've got to talk to each other, tell him how you feel. Have you ever thought that he's maybe just waiting for you to tell him to pack it all in and just live a life of leisure? He has nothing to prove to you after all.'

'Maybe he has something to prove to himself. He wants to succeed in life and the thing is — ' This time she stopped herself. She and Tom had tacitly agreed that nothing was to be said about the perilous state of the business.

Moira reached for the bottle. 'Have another drink. We can talk about it again tomorrow if you want. We can talk on the way over to Mother's.'

'Don't say anything to her. I don't want to worry her.'

'My lips are sealed. Now, let's give it a rest. Never talk about important stuff when you are tired and we have to keep our strength up for tomorrow night. I hope you'll stay to the bitter end.'

'I wouldn't miss it for the world.'

'Thanks for coming. It means a lot to Louisa. It means a lot to me too.'

'I'm looking forward to it. I've bought her a silk dressing-gown. Do you think she'll like it?'

'She'll love it. Thanks. I just hope it all goes off without a hitch. You know what Mum's like and she's already muttering about the no smoking thing. We'll pop over first thing and help her to choose what to wear.'

'She'll wear what *she* wants. I know she's getting on but we mustn't start treating her like a child, Moira.'

'I know. Sorry. As for those two husbands of ours, we shouldn't let them upset us either. Silly buggers.'

'Yes. If it's not one thing it's another with them but they're being very good so far, aren't they?'

'So far but it could kick off anytime.' Moira slipped off her shoes and tucked her legs up under her. 'It's odd, I suppose, that they've both ended up in the same business. Jim's doing very well. On a smaller scale of course.'

Angela glanced at her sharply but she saw from Moira's expression that no dig was intended. 'I'm glad to hear it. What about you? How's the cleaning doing?'

'Fine. I enjoy it. I can't believe how it's blossomed. There really is a need for cleaners, you know, now that nearly every woman goes out to work. Even when people are feeling the pinch they are reluctant to sack the cleaner. I don't earn a fortune but it's all right.'

'I need to do something.' Angela sipped her wine. It was a little sweet but pleasant enough. 'But I don't know what.'

'Buy a shop or something.'

She sighed. 'Why does everybody tell me to do that? I don't want to buy a shop. I can imagine nothing worse.'

'Well then, if you can't get him to give up the business, get involved yourself. Or just start enjoying yourself. Why not go over to the villa more often? You could go on your own if Tom's too busy. Give yourself something to do. Redecorate it, refurnish it or something and learn the language.'

'We don't have the villa any more,' she said, forgetting the warning not to talk about things that matter when you are tired. 'Tom's sold it. He sold it without telling me. In fact, Moira . . . ' she sighed. 'The silly thing is we have a bit of a cashflow problem at the moment.'

'Never.' Moira laughed before she saw that

Angela was not joining in. 'Have you really?'

'It's not only that.' Angela glanced at the clock. They had ages before the men would be back and she should grasp the opportunity and talk to Moira. Quickly, in case she was interrupted mid-way through she gave Moira an outline of the troubles they were having. And then, at the end, she found herself telling her about Cheryl when she had vowed never ever to tell a soul.

Moira listened, let her finish.

'Wow.' Moira unfolded her legs and sat up. 'I'm sure it will get sorted out. I remember Sean vaguely though and he was up to no good when he was twenty so it doesn't sound as if he's changed. Tom should never have trusted him.'

'Don't you think I warned him? But it made no difference. I don't want to say I told you so but I did tell him so.'

'Let me get this Cheryl thing straight: you've been sending this woman money every month? How much?'

'Five hundred.'

'Five hundred pounds a month?' Moira echoed. 'Christ, Angela. Are you mad? For five years? That's over ten thousand a year.'

'I know. It's a lot, but I had half a million in the account. It's all relative. You mustn't tell Tom. He doesn't know.'

'I won't tell him, not if you don't want me to, but I — '

'We threw most of the begging letters out, but I held onto just the one and started to write to her and she's a friend now. She has this autistic son and she has such a hard life with him.'

'Tough.'

'You don't know what it's like. She can't take him to the supermarket in case he kicks off. He has to do the same thing over and over or he gets in a state. Do you know that when they go out they must turn right at the gate or he goes daft and often it means going all the way round the block just to keep the peace? He hardly ever notices her, not properly. She gets nothing back from him. She tells him she loves him but he never says it back. Just think how heart-breaking that must be.'

'I sympathize and I'm sorry to be hard, Angela, but it's not your problem. You have to put a stop to it right now. Write and tell her it's all over.'

'I can't do that. We've been writing to each other for five years, Moira. I've told you, we're friends.'

Moira laughed. 'You are too soft by half. If it had been me she wouldn't have got a penny. She's probably invented the whole thing.'

Angela shook her head. 'No, it's all genuine. I'm sure of it. I can't write a letter saying it's over. I can't tell her that there'll be no more money.'

'You have no choice. Tom's going to find out isn't he, when there isn't as much in your account as he thinks?'

'I could just say I spent it on clothes. He won't query it.'

'Then what's the problem?'

'I don't want to lie about it any more. I'm tired of it. I need to confess.'

'You poor thing,' Moira sighed. 'What it is to have a conscience! We all tell lies, love, and you could easily spend five hundred a month on clothes. Even I could given the chance. You're not fit to have money either of you. God, Angie, I can't believe Tom invested in such a crackpot scheme. He should have talked to me. I would have told him to steer well away from it.'

'Don't you think I did that? And our financial man was adamant he shouldn't touch it, but it didn't make a scrap of difference. And how could he come to you and admit that something was wrong? He has his pride.'

'Stuff that. Look, one thing at a time. If you want rid of this Cheryl woman then you have no alternative but to tell her it's over. Why

184

don't I come with you to see her and you can talk to her and explain it all? She'll have to try her luck with another lottery winner. Either that or get a job like everybody else.' Her laugh was brittle. 'What on earth prompted you to send cash? I can't believe you sent all that money through the post?'

'It's surprising how small a bundle it is. It fits into a big padded envelope,' Angela told her, thinking back now and remembering that it was Cheryl who had suggested cash rather than a cheque. Tom might query a regular cheque, she had said, which had seemed likely at the time although in fact he never opened her letters and had never so much as glanced at her personal bank statements, being of no interest to him at all.

'I never send money through the post, not even a ten pound note,' Moira shook her head. 'You've been a pushover, Angie. What a nice little extra earner for her each month. You can bet your sweet life she won't be declaring your money to the tax man and I wouldn't be surprised if she's claiming benefits as well. People like her know how to milk the system.'

'She hasn't had a holiday for years. She lives in this little house and she tries really hard to keep it nice for her and Richard. Owning a car is out of the question. I did think of buying her one but — '

'Give me strength. Thank God you didn't.'

'You don't know anything about her.' Angela said defiantly.

'Neither do you.'

But she did. She had all the letters. She knew all about the family and all about Cheryl's early life with that abusive father who ended up in jail and that pathetic sounding mother. She knew about Cheryl's unfortunate choice in men and the callous way her last bloke walked out on her when he realized that Richard was going to need a lot of care and attention for the rest of his life. Cheryl's sisters lived in Glasgow and Leeds respectively and had families of their own to cope with so she didn't see much of them. Her sister Jackie was expecting a new baby due in September and Cheryl had told her about the cute little outfit she had bought, neutral because they hadn't found out if it was a boy or girl. Last Christmas she and Richard had been invited to spend it with her brother Mark down in Kent but then the snow came and they couldn't make the long bus trip so they ended up spending Christmas Day on their own, just the two of them and Richard had thrown one of his spectacular tantrums in the middle of the Queen's speech because she had put the wrong number of peas on his plate. Yes, she even had to count the peas. Richard could count them in an instant.

Poor Cheryl, having to live with that. It made her own problems with Melanie seem so little. But the harsh truth was they were facing a dilemma and she might have to subsidize Tom with some money and thereafter make some big adjustments to their finances if they were to avoid having a large-scale panic, so there was no real choice. Belt tightening meant sacrifices and she was sure Cheryl would understand. She was not giving her a huge amount, not in the scheme of things, but it was just another thing to tot up and it was the bits they were spending here there and everywhere that needed to be drastically pruned.

'We'll go to see her if you like and then we can tell her nicely face to face,' Moira said. 'We'll take her some flowers and a final little present. I'm sure she will be very understanding. She must have known it wouldn't go on forever.'

'Does that mean you're going to come with me?' Angela smiled with relief.

'Of course. What are sisters for?'

14

Tom and Jim rolled in later. Not too drunk but obviously having had a few so that they were merry.

There was no sign of the girls but Louisa had her key and would ring if there was a problem.

'You seem to be getting on well with Jim,' Angela remarked as they finally tumbled into bed. She was exhausted and did not know why because she had done very little today. Perhaps it was the effect of finally getting things out in the open, of telling Moira the secret she had harboured for years, and of finally having someone tell her the truth about it.

Maybe she had been naïve. Maybe, and she hated the thought, maybe Cheryl was a fraud although she found that hard to believe. Moira was worldly wise though in a way she had never been and she was glad that she was on her side. She knew she would not tell a soul.

Tom reached for her clumsily but she gently but firmly rebuffed him. She was having none of that, not in her sister's bed.

'For God's sake, Angie,' he murmured against her hair. 'It's been ages.'

For her certainly but what about him? Who was he cuddling up to on those nights away?

'You smell of booze,' she told him coldly. 'Goodnight. We've got a busy day tomorrow.'

★　★　★

She awoke in the early hours, hearing agitated voices, the sound of running heels up the path, the key in the lock, a light showing under the bedroom door.

'Mum . . . ' It was Louisa's voice, coming nearer.

The door opened after a quick knock and Angela sat up blinking.

'Oh sorry, I forgot . . . ' She was heading out again then stopped. 'Aunty Angie, there's been an accident. It's Melanie.'

'Is she all right?' Trying to take it in, she heard her own voice dimly from afar as if she was still sleeping.

'They've taken her to hospital. She fell downstairs at the club,' Louisa said, *her* voice scared. 'Top to bottom. She tripped in those heels. She banged her head.'

'But is she *all right*?' Angela was yelling at her now as Moira emerged from the floor above. She was wearing the most Godawful

189

shapeless cotton pyjamas, hair standing on end and looked fat, Angela thought, in a sudden irrational moment. Down in the hall, she now saw a strange young man standing there.

'Who the hell's that?' Moira asked the question, still befuddled from sleep.

'Leo.' Louisa dismissed him. 'We have to go to the hospital.'

'Why didn't you ring us?' Moira was standing there, only slowing coming to. Angela wondered if she looked the same, dizzy still with sleep.

'Because I didn't want to tell you something like this over the *phone*,' Louisa was now exasperated. 'Are you coming or what?'

For the first time Angela noticed the blood on Louisa's dress causing her maternal alarm bells to ring out loudly.

'What's going on? Why is everybody up?' Tom appeared, dressing-gowned and yawning.

'It's Melanie,' Angela said, stirred into action and heading firstly for some clothes and then the car.

★ ★ ★

They were jammed into Angela's car heading for the nearest hospital, a good thirty minute drive away following the closure — after a prolonged but ultimately useless protest — of their local A&E department.

Angela was driving with Tom beside her and in the back Moira, Louisa and Leo, Melanie's blind date. Jim had stayed at home because they thought somebody ought to remain there. Terry Banner was at the hospital with Melanie. Louisa had been shivering uncontrollably standing there in the blood-spattered dress and Moira had hastily grabbed a jacket for her, an old anorak with a fur-lined hood that, designed for Arctic conditions, looked ridiculous over the flimsy dress.

The story was coming out in panicky bursts, Louisa only just managing to hold it together which surprised Moira because she was usually so calm in an emergency. Things were winding down at the disco and people were drifting off when it happened. After the initial mayhem, qualified first-aiders were immediately on the scene rushing down to join Louisa and Terry at the foot of the steps where Melanie lay. Her body was twisted awkwardly and she was out cold for a worrying few seconds, bleeding from the head. Somebody, Terry in fact, had taken off his jacket and laid it across her. The ambulance had come promptly and the paramedics had attended to her before eventually loading her on a stretcher into the ambulance, setting off with lights flashing.

'There was a lot of blood,' Louisa whispered to Moira, looking as if all the blood had drained out of *her*. 'Don't tell Aunty Angela that.'

It was the flashing blue lights that worried Moira the most for that signified urgency. After they had all dressed in ten minutes flat, there was some daft argument as to whose car they should use although Moira's heap was scarcely big enough for all of them. Angela insisted she was fine to drive and Moira had to agree. For somebody who was irritatingly submissive about most things, Angela was the most confident and able driver she knew. She had to be to manoeuvre it out of the tight space she had miraculously backed into.

Moira, after making a quick call to accident and emergency, was last in the car, belting up even as Angela set off.

'I hope Mel wasn't drunk,' Moira whispered to Louisa. 'Tell me now if she was.'

'No. We didn't drink much. It was those stupid heels that did it. Just as we were passing the steps she tripped over her dress and couldn't keep her balance. I tried to stop her, tore her dress and very nearly went with her.'

Moira recalled the ankle-length dress, a designer label Melanie had been quick to tell them, although she thought Louisa looked just as nice in her high street number. She remembered the way they had looked, Melanie, her blonde hair carefully dishevelled, sparkling diamond ear-rings, dark eyes shining too and Louisa, her blonde hair straight and sleek wearing her halter-necked pink dress. In a perfect world Louisa could pass a few pounds over to her cousin and then they would both be the right size. They had set off, behaving like the teenagers they still were, thrilled at the prospect of the blind date.

The blind date in question was sitting beside Moira and she had ascertained although he had answered with scared eyes, that he was Leo Potter.

'Any relation to Harry?' she asked, trying in vain for some light relief.

'Who?'

She gave up when Louisa nudged her. All right, she was just trying to keep them all calm, that was all. Leo seemed stunned and she could not get a further word out of him although, unable to stop herself and to try to keep things on an ordinary footing in this most extraordinary of situations, she tried some maternally probing questions to find out more about him, where he lived, did he have any brothers and sisters, what he did for a living and so on, until she realized that it hardly mattered and she would probably never set eyes on him again. He was shocked, poor soul, and seemed temporarily to have lost the ability to speak.

'Don't worry, Leo,' she told him, patting his knee. 'It wasn't your fault.'

'It might have been. We were fooling around.'

'What?' She smiled at him, wondering where they had dragged him up from. He had not shaved for some time, or perhaps he was aiming for the interesting designer stubble look of some male models. In his case it wasn't working and in addition he reeked of some aftershave that she wasn't particularly fond of.

'We were fooling around so it wasn't really an accident. If we hadn't been fooling around it would never have happened.'

'Now, Leo, we can't go around saying things like that,' she said in a stern mummy-voice. 'Don't start blaming yourself. She tripped and fell down the stairs.'

'Yeah, I suppose that's what happened.'

'Well then, it *was* an accident.'

She sighed.

On her other side, Louisa was texting

194

wildly but Terry was not answering. Quite why Terry had opted to stay with Melanie had not been explained, but Moira found she was not surprised. She was beginning to realize that there was more to Terry than she had first thought. Now she had to add *caring* to the list of his attributes. He was not the sort of young man to abandon a sick female to her fate. She was warming to Terry and she should stop being a snob and thinking that he wasn't good enough for her daughter. She would not raise any objections to their continuing relationship and, if it did manage to survive, then well and good. He could always be a house-husband and look after the kids, fitting in the electrical stuff when he could whilst Louisa did her doctoring. She had no doubt now that he would make an excellent daddy.

'His mobile's switched off,' Louisa said, dropping the phone into her bag. She was pale and tense and Moira reached for her hand to give it an encouraging squeeze although, to her surprise, Louisa responded by withdrawing it with a shudder of irritation.

'I don't think mobiles are encouraged in hospital,' Angela said suddenly, breaking a silence from the front. If she didn't know better Tom looked as if he had drifted off again but she discounted that thought

195

immediately as he half turned and tried to smile at her. 'We must not read anything into it,' Angela continued briskly. 'They did say it wasn't life-threatening, didn't they? You are telling me the truth, Moira?'

'Of course I am. They're doing a scan just to make sure but don't worry, Angie, she'll be fine. A bit sore maybe but she's not going to die.'

'Sometimes you are OK at first but they have to watch you because you can take a turn for the worse for no reason,' Leo piped up, unexpectedly and unhelpfully. 'That can happen with head injuries and especially with young fit people. There can be a sudden bleed. A mate of mine was riding this motorbike over at Coniston and he had this accident. He tried to overtake on a bend and wham . . . ended up skewed across the road.'

Everybody collectively held their breath.

'They took him to hospital and he was sitting up in bed saying he was OK and everybody thought he'd been lucky but then that night — '

'Not now, Leo.' Moira hissed at him, digging him sharply in the ribs. Who did he think he was, some sort of consultant neurologist?

'You didn't all need to come along,' Tom

said with a trace of irritation. 'They won't let us all in.'

'We're here to support *you*,' Moira said firmly, smiling at the back of his head and recalling with a sudden vivid clarity the moment Melanie was born. Tom was wearing that same anxious look and she hoped that, whatever their problems were, he and Angela would sort them out. He loved her sister and not her and it was time she got over it and let go of the Tom that was, that handsome young boy, her very first love. She loved Jim, her solid dependable unromantic man and teenage fixations had no place in the life of a middle-aged mother.

'Where is this fucking hospital?' Angela said suddenly, approaching a junction.

At Moira's side, Louisa gasped and even Moira was shocked for she had never before heard Angela swear let alone utter *that* word, which brought it home just how worried she was. Until she saw and talked to her daughter, she was not going to believe the soothing words of some woman on the telephone. And she wished the blind date had kept his mouth shut. Where the hell had they dug him up from? She hadn't got a word out of him and then when he did speak it was to upset the applecart completely and worry them all sick.

'We're nearly there. Take a right here.' Calmly Moira directed her to the entrance and Angela, blithely ignoring their half-hearted protests, pulled into a space reserved for the disabled.

They scrambled out and set off.

Considering they had dressed hurriedly, the two of them looked great, Moira thought as she followed them, realizing that her own choice of emergency garments — grey jogging pants, trainers and an old sweatshirt — were not in the same league. Angela was wearing slim fitting jeans and a crisp white blouse with a navy silk tie-front cardigan and toning navy and white sandals, a navy bag slung over her shoulder. Even in the depths of despair as she had been it seemed that she was still capable of colour co-ordination.

Moira, her purse stuffed in the track-suit bottoms, looked and felt very much like the poor relation.

But then, that is exactly what she was.

Oh come on, get a grip. What was she doing worrying about something so petty at a time like this?

Smiling encouragingly at Louisa who was still worryingly pale she held open the door for Leo as acres of corridors and the hospital smell came at them like a tsunami.

The verdict was as good as it gets. No bones broken. No lasting damage. Just scrapes and bruises and a cut head which had been stitched.

She had been extremely lucky, the doctor told them and, although they could keep her overnight to monitor her, she was happy enough for them to take her home. A few days' rest was suggested — not a problem for Melanie — and, of course, if there were any problems with vision or dizziness they were to take her straight to her GP.

'Thank you so much, Doctor.' Angela could have kissed her and was so relieved that at that moment she would willingly have written a huge cheque to provide a new high tech machine or something but Melanie was already being led away and she needed to catch up.

She read nothing into the fact that Louisa's boyfriend had his arm around Melanie, that Melanie was leaning prettily against him, that Louisa's face was tightly controlled, that Moira was looking at her questioningly.

Leo wanted to take a taxi home and Tom fished out a twenty-pound note for the fare, dismissing the boy's attempts to find some change for him. They found a taxi and waved him off.

They dropped Terry off at his house, Melanie kissing him on the cheek and tearfully thanking him for staying with her before returning to Moira's house which was lit up like a Christmas tree, where Jim was waiting.

Hugs of relief all round.

★　★　★

'Do you want some hot milk, darling?' Angela had reverted to mummy mode, helping a shaken and sore Melanie get undressed and into her silk pyjamas and then practically tucking her daughter into the narrow bed. 'And would you like me to sit with you for a while?'

'Yes, please.'

Everybody had dispersed to their beds by the time she came back with the hot milk, Melanie propped up in the bed with its pretty striped duvet cover. Contrary to her worst fears, the duvet and the pillows were of excellent quality fit for a princess. The clock on the bedside table said 2.30 and Angela yawned, pulling a chair over so that the two of them could talk, if Melanie felt up to it of course.

'You scared me, sweetheart,' she said, half expecting Melanie to brush away the hand she was offering. But no, Melanie took hold of it and gripped it a moment, leaning back against the heaped pillows. Her make-up was still on although much depleted but this was no time for the evening cosmetic routine that Melanie normally indulged in. For once she could manage without.

'I scared myself,' Melanie admitted, touching her head gingerly. 'Will I have terrible bruises?'

'A few. But they will fade.'

'You know what it's like when it's in slow motion. I knew I couldn't stop it; I knew I was going to go down those steps. Those bloody shoes . . . they're ruined you know and they cost me five hundred quid. And I tore the hem of my dress,' she finished with a wail.

'Hems can be fixed and we can buy a new pair of shoes,' Angela told her gently, speaking low so as not to disturb anybody. There was a street lamp outside so it was not completely dark, not the black-out darkness that they experienced at home when the bay disappeared into a silky dark hole and the only glow was from moonlight. The outside lamp cast a soft glow round the room, one wall papered in a vibrant floral design, the carpet a soft apple green. And, as it was a large room, Moira had found space for an office corner but it did not look incongruous in the least, looked as if it was meant to be there. My goodness, Moira could teach Megan a thing or two.

'She hates me, Mum.' Melanie blew on the milk, hands cupping the mug. Seeing the mark of the stitches and the stain on her blonde hair Angela felt a maternal pull such as she had not felt for some time. 'I can't help it, can I, if a boy fancies me?'

'But that was the idea,' Angela told her with a smile. 'You're lucky. He seemed nice although he didn't say a lot, but I'm sure he was very concerned about your accident.' She decided not to mention the bit about his mate with the motor bike whose fate they could all guess. 'All the blind dates I ever had were complete disasters.'

'It wasn't Leo, he's a complete nerd. It was Terry,' she said. 'He was the one who fancied me. And the thing is I really like him too. I can't help it, can I, if he was going out with Louisa? They aren't engaged or anything and he's only been going out with her a few weeks.'

'Oh, darling, what are you saying?'

'Terry fancies me and he's made that very plain. Mum, he took me aside to tell me that and he was just so sweet.'

'For heaven's sake, Mel, you couldn't have picked a worse time. It's her birthday tomorrow . . . today . . . ' she corrected herself. 'What's going to happen at the party now? I hope that he's going to stay away, or it will be just too awkward. Did he say anything?'

'About what? There was no need for explanations. It wasn't serious with Louisa. It was pretty obvious the minute we set eyes on each other. Oh Mum, have you ever been in love?' She smiled. 'Of course you have. So you know all about it. We took one look at each other and that was it and that was why he came with me to the hospital. He couldn't bear to leave me alone and he held my hand in the ambulance and everything. I thought I was going to bleed to death but they said you always get a lot of blood from a head wound.'

Angela stroked her hair, carefully avoiding the wound. She had always been a drama queen.

'Well, I think we should all get some sleep now and just forget it for the moment. I'm sure that you're right and Terry was just Louisa's friend, nothing more than that. There's no reason to suppose it would be serious with you either. Remember he knows who you are and — '

'It's not about my money,' she interrupted sharply. 'Why must it always be about the money? Why do you think that every single boy I go out with is just after my money? They might like *me*, Mum. In any case, Louisa won't exactly be short either when she reaches twenty-five. Terry can't lose either way and I'm afraid I beat her hands down in the looks department. Well I do, don't I? She's going to be fat if she doesn't watch it. She'll have to spend some of her money when she gets it on a breast reduction,' she said, as Angela shushed her, afraid her suddenly rising voice might be overheard. 'She hates me,' she repeated.

'No she does not and I won't have any more of that.' Angela adjusted the cover suddenly feeling very tired. 'You two are like sisters and sisters don't hate each other.'

'But she pushed me, Mum.'

'What did you say?' Angela had been edging out of the room but was stopped short.

'Louisa pushed me down those stairs.'

Quickly, she returned to Melanie's bedside. 'Do you realize what you are saying?'

'She pushed me, Mum. Cross my heart and hope to die.' She made a feeble effort to do just that. 'I felt her hand on my back just before I fell.'

'Goodness me, Melanie, you can't go around making accusations like that. Don't you dare repeat that to anybody. That is real mischief making and you have to stop it right away.'

'You don't believe me, do you?' Tears filled her eyes. 'Just because I kept quiet about it, didn't say a word until now, just because I told them at the hospital it was an accident, you don't believe me. You think I'm making it up.'

'I think you're suffering from delayed shock, Melanie love, and it can make you say silly things.'

'She was so jealous when she saw Terry was ignoring her that she clammed up for the whole night and then, as we were coming out she made me trip up and fall down those stairs. Leo knows. He tried to stop me falling. It was Leo who tore my dress, not Louisa.'

'Nobody *made* you trip up. It was those shoes. They were designed to trip you up. Now, let's have no more of this. Go to sleep now. And you're not to repeat what you've just said to anybody. It could cause real trouble. This has got to stay between just me and you. Promise?'

She repeated the word as Melanie snuggled down and closed her eyes.

'I promise,' Melanie said softly.

'Love you.' Angela kissed her gently and, after a final check that she was settling down, she closed the door behind her.

Slipping back into bed and putting her cold feet on her husband's warm ones, she recalled that much the same thing had happened when she met Tom for he had been Moira's boyfriend briefly before he was hers.

It was not her fault just as it was not Melanie's fault.

Yes, Tom had gone out with Moira and because it was a small town they had all gone to the same school although it was surprising how tight your own circle of friends was and how little you knew of the people on the circumference.

For the first few weeks then that Moira and Tom were seeing each other, she stayed in the background. There was nothing sinister in it and she was not aware of making a conscious effort to do it, but one day she walked into the living-room where Moira and Tom were cosily entrenched on the sofa. It was early evening and they were probably just exchanging a chaste kiss but they leapt apart pretty quickly and she remembered being embarrassed and making some daft remark before backing out.

That was the beginning of the end for Moira and Tom and for her and Tom it was how it all started. And it was just as Melanie had said: one look was all it took.

Moira did not speak to her for two whole weeks. Their mother said it was up to them to sort it out and she was not taking sides, but Moira was a stubborn soul and although Angela considered ending it because it was causing such hassle she could not bring herself to do it because she loved Tom. She loved the way he smiled, winked at her, those twinkling eyes, the wonderful feeling she had when he held her and kissed her, just everything about him. After two silent weeks, it was her father, surprisingly, who said he had had enough of it and he made them both say sorry as if they were five and six years old again.

'You'll find somebody else,' she remembered saying to Moira, who had given her a look that she had never quite forgotten.

And then thank God Jim came along and before they had time to think Moira was pregnant and getting married.

So, all's well that ends well, or something like that.

She did not want a repeat scenario, although Louisa was not as strong-willed as her mother, a very nice girl who would probably give in gracefully if anything were to come of this.

She was probably worrying about nothing for Terry would no doubt miss the party — if he had any sensitivity whatsoever — and Louisa would bounce back quickly for she was a tough young lady and not the sort to allow a little boyfriend trouble to distract her from enjoying her own birthday. But was Louisa the sort of girl who would push somebody down steep stone steps risking serious injury? She could not believe that of her.

Tom was deeply asleep and she tried to settle, trying to link her breathing to his, but it took some time to go back to sleep and when she did she dreamed of sinister-looking concrete steps and peculiarly of Ron who was in uniform and driving, not their green Jaguar, but a bus and she was sitting on it, counting the coins in her purse, worried that she might not have enough for the return fare.

15

Melanie, in full blown invalid mode, did not surface until 10.30 next morning. Unwisely, Moira had planned a big family sit-down breakfast; juice, a selection of cereals, full English for anybody who wanted it, toast and home-made marmalade and a big pot of coffee. Nobody felt like it although Tom rose to the occasion as he saw her disappointment and said he would love some scrambled eggs and perhaps a couple of rashers of bacon.

'Coming up,' she said happily, thinking that he looked fresher than anybody else this morning. Angela looked awful. As for herself, she had done her best but she had not slept well, worrying about Melanie and hearing a lot of movement on the floor below. That damned Leo and his words of medical wisdom had unsettled her and she was half expecting to be woken urgently with Mel suddenly taking a turn for the worse, haemorrhaging internally and on the brink of death.

Louisa was up early, red-eyed and the worse for wear, asking after Melanie and wondering if she should go in to see how she was.

'Leave her be,' Moira told her, glancing at her but not commenting on the obvious signs of a night spent weeping. 'Will Terry be along later?' she asked.

'I doubt it.' Louisa shrugged. 'It's off.'

'Off?' Why was she not surprised and why was she a little upset when all along she had hoped it would be just a flash in the pan? 'Why is it off?'

'Ask that niece of yours,' she said shortly, picking up a slice of toast and wandering off with it.

Moira's dreams of a family breakfast faded.

★   ★   ★

Angela, looking uncomfortable, apologized to Moira for her language last night, particularly saying *that* word in front of Louisa. 'I can't think what came over me,' she said. 'I very rarely say it. I might think it sometime but I don't say it.'

'Don't be daft. Youngsters aren't the least fazed by it and you have a good excuse because you were out of your mind with worry. And it helps, doesn't it, to let it rip?'

'I suppose so, but Tom doesn't like to hear me swear.'

'Sod Tom.' She put her arm round Angela's shoulder. 'You have to learn to stand up to him, love. You let him treat you like a doormat and that's just not on.'

'Has Louisa said anything about what happened last night?'

'Melanie's accident? Only that it all happened in a flash. These things do, don't they? I once went hell for leather when I caught my foot on the rug. I just missed the edge of the table so there but for the grace of God and all that . . . ' She glanced at her sister. 'Why? Has Melanie remembered anything?'

Angela shook her head and, after checking that nobody was listening, Moira quietly reminded her that the visit to this Cheryl woman was not going to be put off. It was working out quite well because in their new improved relationship — and she must not let this thing with Terry upset that because that was for their daughters to sort out — Angela had suggested a weekend away at a spa hotel near Bath and whilst they were there they would make the time for a detour and visit Cheryl to break the news.

Moira did not anticipate any trouble but, if the woman turned nasty, she would be there to look after her little sister. Angela hated upsetting people and would buckle under the weight of a sob-story.

For the rest of the day she was too busy getting her hair done, producing a makeshift lunch and collecting Dilys to worry about Angela's little problem.

★ ★ ★

Dilys collared Moira in the newly refurbished Ladies at The Queen's Head.

'What's going on?' she asked, plonking her sparkly evening bag down on the tiled shelf and taking out a lipstick. 'Everybody looks as if they've just spent a wet weekend at Rhyl. It's supposed to be a party, isn't it? If it doesn't liven up soon I'm off. Your dad and me always enjoyed a dance but you can't dance to any of this music, if you can call it that.'

'The youngsters don't dance like that any more. It'll all be over in about twenty minutes,' Moira said, privately acknowledging that as parties go it had not been the most exuberant, her mother's earlier enthusiasm in attempting a tango — with Jim of all people — drawing a round of applause and promising to be the highlight of the evening.

She glanced at her mother as she applied her ubiquitous plum lipstick, astonished as always that she could at first glance pass for a woman in her late sixties. She was wearing a silvery-grey calf-length dress with high-heeled shoes and Moira saw that the evening bag contained just four items; the lipstick, a small bottle of her favourite Chanel perfume, a packet of cigarettes and the cigarette lighter. Dilys had complained bitterly that it was a bit off making an old lady like herself stand outside on a cool summer's evening in order to have a smoke.

'It was perishing out there,' she said when she returned. 'I'll catch my death and then they'll know about it. You have my permission, Moira, to sue the pants off them if I pop my clogs.'

On the contrary, she looked as fresh now at half past midnight as she had done when she arrived. There was no stopping her and Moira hoped she would be as lively at that age although, just now, after a bad night's sleep and all the hassle with Melanie who had been the centre of attention all day, she felt close on ninety herself.

Dilys waited until Moira had refreshed her own make-up. 'Melanie has been in the wars I see. She fell down some stairs last night Louisa tells me, and had to be rushed to hospital. That sounds serious. Why wasn't I told? I'm always the last to know anything in this family.'

'I didn't want to worry you, Mum.'

'I'm made of stern stuff, Moira. I don't need things to be kept from me.'

'Sorry. She's fine anyway apart from a sore head and hand.'

'And that's not the only thing: Melanie's only been here five minutes and already she's pinched Louisa's boyfriend. What do you make of that? History repeating itself, eh?'

'Terry's not her boyfriend. He's just a friend. One of many,' she said hastily.

'That's not what she told me. The child's heartbroken.'

'I know, Mum.' Moira sighed. 'But what can I do?'

'Nothing.' Dilys shook her head, a slide sparkling in the white hair. 'Just as I could do nothing all those years ago, Moira, even though you asked me to. I knew as soon as I saw Tom look at Angela that it was all over with you.'

'But it was so sneaky the way she did it,' Moira muttered, hoping nobody would come in whilst they were engaged in this particular topic of conversation. She had to stop blaming Angela for it took two to tango as had just been demonstrated most ably in the ballroom. 'Do you remember that blue Beetle he was so proud of?'

'I do. It had a mind of its own, that car.'

'Well he took *her* out in it but he never took me,' she said, knowing as her mother laughed that it was one of the most childish things she had uttered in ages. 'I kept asking him to take me out in his car but he never did and then, when he'd only been going out with Angie for a few weeks he took her out to Blackpool for the day and *she* didn't even ask him,' she added, the memory vivid. Angela had looked terrific in a red coat and new black boots and she had watched her clambering into the car from behind the curtain, shaking with rage and jealousy.

'Blackpool? I can't stand that place. Give me Morecambe any day. Your dad used to take me there. You can see right across the bay to the hills. And the air is so special. It's not bracing like Blackpool, it's soporific.'

'Is it indeed?' Moira, despite the memory, managed a smile.

'You mustn't let it get to you, sweetheart.'

She rarely called her that these days.

'Oh Mum, I had such plans for us.' She stopped short of telling her mother that, on one of their nights out together she had been the first person to know about his plans for starting up his painting and decorating business using a bit of money he had from his grandfather. Even as she listened and encouraged, she was already deciding on the

215

names for their children.

'The thing is . . . ' Dilys's voice gentled. 'You can't *make* a man love you and that's a fact, but in any relationship there's always one of you who loves that little bit more than the other and that's a fact too. Your father loved me more than I did him. He worshipped the ground I walked on and sometimes I treated him like dirt and I regret that now.'

'Honestly, Mum, I wish you wouldn't say things like that. You don't mean it.'

'Don't tell me what I do and do not mean. Doesn't Tom look nice?' she switched the subject in an instant. 'That colour is lovely on him. And did you see that ring of Angela's? I bet that cost a mint.'

'I expect it did.' Moira zipped up her bag and fussed a minute with her hair, reluctant to go back into the room for the final straight because you could cut the atmosphere in there with a knife. She hoped it wasn't obvious to anybody else for Louisa was doing her best not to show her disappointment. Terry was clinging to Melanie like a limpet and Melanie, miraculously recovered, was playing up to him for all she was worth. She was not allowed to dance, nothing lively anyway, but had managed to drag herself onto the dance floor for a slow number putting her head on Terry's sturdy shoulder, insinuating her body into his and coming as close to making love on the dance-floor as it was possible to do.

It had stopped people in their tracks.

Frankly she hadn't been able to take her eyes off the pair of them, remembering with an ache in her heart the few times she had danced a slow number with Tom; at those parties at Christmas and New Year to be precise before Angela appeared on the scene, flashed those gorgeous dark eyes at him, tossed that glossy mane, and nicked him. She had not spoken to her for two whole weeks before she saw that she was not doing herself any favours and so, shaking off her disappointment and throwing herself at a somewhat surprised Jim had been the ultimate of I'll-show-you gestures.

'You can do better than that Jim,' her mother had said and she still believed it.

She was nineteen years old when Tom left her for Angela and never in a million years had she thought that a couple of years on she would be a wife and mother. Four months pregnant with Adele, squeezed into a white wedding dress it was a low-key affair, her mother silently unforgiving, her wedding day face a picture, but her dad hugging her and telling her that he had no doubts that Jim would look after her. There was nothing wrong with Jim, he said.

Just imagine that she had at first likened Terry to Jim.

He wasn't fit to wipe Jim's boots.

She had revised her opinion of that young man; insensitive and money-grabbing was added to the list just as caring and thoughtful were crossed out. He was quite obviously out for what he could get and she was annoyed she had been taken in by him in the first place. Jim was blissfully unaware of anything amiss, but Angela had certainly taken note and she caught her anxious look a couple of times and was therefore avoiding her. The fact that the relationship between Louisa and Terry was over before it had properly begun stirred her protective instincts nonetheless and she was hard pressed not to say something. For a kick-off nobody in their right mind would be crass enough to actually come along this evening when his presence would plainly make things unbearable for the party girl. Melanie ought to know better, too, but then she was singularly selfish these days.

With a full blown shouting match out of the question, she was making do in the meantime with murderous looks aimed at Terry, but they were having little effect. The cheery smile and little wave he directed her way were frankly unbelievable, only serving to confirm, of course, that he was just like his father; a little short in the sensitivity department.

Out in the function room, things were winding down. The refreshment table looked like a bomb had landed in it, above it the pink balloons were deflating, streamers were sagging, people looking slightly the worse for wear and wondering when they could decently leave, the waiting staff standing around ready to spring into action, and the DJ now a little desperate as people lost interest. Jim was nowhere to be seen and Louisa, still brightly smiling, was in line for an Oscar for best actress of the evening.

The formalities had been attended to. They had cut the cake earlier and sung 'Happy Birthday' followed by the unseemly rush to the refreshment table. After that, whilst the DJ stuffed himself with sausage rolls, Tom had virtually elbowed Jim aside and stepped up to say a few words which had infuriated Moira because Jim, although reluctant, had nevertheless been practising a short speech.

And then, definitely not on the agenda, Louisa had insisted on saying a few words herself, a few heartfelt and moving words of thanks to her and Jim for eighteen happy years and how grateful she was to them for giving her the opportunity to go to university and how she hoped to make them proud of her, choking a bit at the last which had nearly set Moira off too. She looked so pretty standing there in her blue dress, her hair up, wearing her new ear-rings but as Moira glanced round at the assembled guests she caught sight of Melanie and Terry sitting close together and laughing, Melanie looking none the worse for what she was calling her near-death experience. Near death, my eye.

She wished Adele was here but she couldn't have everything and soon, when Louisa was gone, it would be back to square one with just the two of them, her and Jim and it was then, at that moment when the nest was empty, that it could go either way. She both looked forward to and dreaded it.

After Louisa finished her piece, Jim, speech stuffed in his pocket, had looked at her questioningly but she shook her head because enough was enough and the moment had passed for him to say anything.

⋆ ⋆ ⋆

The numbers were diminishing as people began to leave but, of course, as hosts they were obliged to stay on until the bitter end.

'Just hang around for a minute or two and

see people off, would you?' she asked Jim. 'I just need a few minutes on my own.'

'To do what?'

She did not answer, already heading for the small quiet lounge which she knew would be completely empty at this hour. She wanted to sit down and sort out in her head what on earth was going on with Louisa before she slipped up and said the wrong thing to her. Eighteen-year-old girls needed to be handled with extreme caution, she knew that, and although she was putting on a good show of not caring a fly's fart for Terry, Moira knew her own daughter too well to know it was just that: an act. It was also just a little upsetting that she had chosen to open up to her grandmother rather than Moira.

Closing the door of the lounge quietly, she thought there was nobody there until Tom spoke, half hidden behind the high backed sofa.

'Is that you, Sister-in-law?'

The tone was mocking and she wondered how much he had had to drink,

'What are you doing here?' she asked, going round and finding him lolling there. 'Sit up straight,' she told him, annoyed even as she said it because she was not his mother for goodness sake and who was she to tell him what to do?

He sat up straight anyway, glass in hand, and smiled at her, patting the seat beside him. 'Come and sit down,' he said. 'Don't worry, I'm sober as a judge.'

'Really?' she hesitated, not prepared to argue the point. He was not drunk, but he had had enough and his eyes were bright. He was certainly not fit to drive, not that he would be doing that for some time yet. 'We're going in a minute,' she told him. 'The DJ's down to the last few and then he will be packing up.'

'Come and sit down,' he repeated, smile widening. 'Don't tell me you're scared of me.'

'Now why on earth would I be scared of you, Tom?' she asked, having no option but to do as he asked, sitting on the sofa and smoothing down the skirt of her midnight-blue dress. It was her second choice but it fitted well, the front daringly cut for her but what the hell. Sometimes you needed to feel like a woman instead of just a wife and mother and the new push-up bra was worth every penny. She had the matching knickers, too, and had planned a surprise for Jim when they got home but, following the downbeat nature of the party, she was rapidly going off that idea.

'Don't tell me you don't remember when it was just the two of us,' he said, his hand trailing across the back of the sofa and somehow ending up along her shoulders. 'I remember, darling.'

'You *are* drunk,' she said lightly, but he put his hand on her chin and turned her face to his and it was impossible then not to look into his eyes. Damn him. They were very close, kissing distance, and it was taking all her strength not to give in, to melt against him, to have him kiss her again. They had never actually gone the whole hog, not in those far-off days mainly because she had been shit-scared of becoming pregnant — ironic really — but there had been some pretty hot moments between them and of course she remembered every single detail.

'There's something about you, Moira Brierley, there's always been something about you.'

'Moira *Rayner*,' she corrected him primly, even though her heart was pounding.

'Jim's a lucky man. I've always found you bloody attractive,' he said at last. As he smiled and drew away she saw in his eyes a sudden retreat and knew that there would be no kiss, not tonight, not ever. 'I'm sorry for ditching you.'

'Don't be. It was never going anywhere,' she said, the lie smarting on her lips.

'I love Angela. I'm not sure she loves me

just now but I love her very much.'

Stone cold sober he would never dream of making such an announcement and it was a bit late to be apologizing for ditching her nearly thirty years ago but he was heart-warmingly sincere as in the way of the slightly tipsy.

'And I love Jim. You are a bastard, Tom.' She tried to control her ragged breathing, to damp down the desire which had ripped through her, moving away just in time as the door opened and she heard her husband's voice.

'There you are, love. I've been looking all over for you.'

She stood up, shakily, adjusting her dress, and Tom called out a cheery greeting to Jim. She felt guilty as hell for Jim must surely guess for she just knew she was flushed, eyes sparkling and for anybody with an ounce of awareness the reason must be obvious.

Jim stood by the door waiting for her to join him, smiling as she did so. 'Tired, darling?'

She returned his smile as, opening the door for her, he followed her out. If he suspected anything he was not going to admit it. But that was Jim. He knew when to leave well alone. Tom was right. She was damned lucky to have him.

She remembered the comment her mother had made, about one person always loving that little bit more.

How true.

★ ★ ★

She needed to concentrate her mind on other things and Dilys, chatting nineteen to the dozen, obliged during the taxi trip back to her house. Moira asked the taxi driver to wait a minute and escorted her mother inside. She had the heating switched on even though it was summer and it felt cloyingly hot.

'Are you sure you'll be all right, Mum?' she asked. 'Do you want me to wait until you get into bed?'

'No. I can sort myself out.' She yawned, stepping out of the silver shoes and suddenly looking her age. 'Off you go. Don't keep that taxi driver waiting. The meter will be ticking.'

'I'll ring you tomorrow.'

'Forget Tom, Moira,' she said softly. 'He's not so bad, that husband of yours. He can do a half decent tango at that. Your father liked Jim and he told me not to worry because he knew that Jim would always be there for you and there's something to be said for that.'

My goodness, everybody was in a very philosophical mood tonight.

She waited until they were home before she questioned Louisa about Terry. They had left Angela and Tom and Jim waiting around for another taxi. There must be a rush on them at this time of night and they were not yet back.

'I know you've been talking to Grandma but you can talk to me about it. Is there anything you want to tell me about him?'

'There's nothing to talk about. Melanie's nailed him. It was so pathetic. The moment she set eyes on him he got the full works and you know her, she always gets what she wants.'

'But she's so thin,' she said, puzzled because she remembered Tony's words. '*And she has a tattoo,*' she added. 'I thought he didn't like tattoos.'

'That's what he told me but I'm not sure I can believe anything that he said. It's no big deal. It was never serious, Mum, so she's welcome to him. I mustn't let anything or anybody get in the way of what I want to do and I'm going to be very busy for the next few years. I really haven't time for a relationship.'

'That's my girl.' She gave her a hug, heart aching for her as she felt her daughter's body trembling beneath her hands knowing that for two pins she would dissolve into tears.

Just then, mercifully maybe, everybody

trailed into the kitchen, over tired and now jaded in their party finery and, taking brisk orders for tea, coffee or chocolate she started getting mugs out of the cupboard. Melanie was absent, she noticed, but she had no wish to know where she was or what she was up to. She had enjoyed the attention she had tonight, wounded soldier and all that, playing up to it for all she was worth even to the extent of affecting a sympathy-inducing limp.

Little minx.

16

Back home, Tom had an uncomfortable feeling he had come close to making a fool of himself with Moira. He had been a bit the worse for wear and vaguely he recalled sitting beside her on a sofa. She had been wearing a dress that moulded itself to her figure and she looked bright and pretty, her brown eyes more cappuccino than Angela's dark chocolate and he might have said more than he meant to. Fortunately that was as far as it went and Jim had interrupted them before she pounced on him.

He didn't think he was flattering himself because he knew damned well they had always had feelings for each other although they were of the playful variety on his part and not at all the much deeper feelings he felt for Angela.

He would have to steer well clear of his dear sister-in-law in future.

He did not have the opportunity to dwell on it because he had requested a meeting with Charles Grey and Charles arrived at the house just missing Angela who was out for lunch. Charles suggested that they wait until she was back so that she could sit in on it but Tom thought it better if he just reported back to her.

'She knows we're in some trouble so this is not going to be a surprise,' he explained, as he took Charles through to his study. As requested beforehand, Ron's wife appeared as soon as they were settled, bringing in coffee and biscuits.

'Thanks, Annie,' he said with a smile which she returned, a little oddly, before leaving them to it.

He needed rescuing. He was hoping against hope that Charles would be his knight in shining armour. Charles took his time, accepting a cup of coffee, black no sugar, and sitting there in his pinstripe three-piece suit, white shirt and silk tie. He had a superior and slightly sinister look about him with an aquiline nose, his greying hair curling on his collar.

'Let's have it then.' Charles glanced at his watch, one to rival Tom's. Tom noted the tan leather shoes, able to spot quality footwear now. He reached for one of Mrs Ron's homemade biscuits before deciding against it. This was serious and he did not want to be at a disadvantage trying to talk numbers through a mouthful of crumbs. Charles declined the biscuits, too, but then he didn't look as if he had eaten a biscuit in his life.

Charles listened as Tom went quickly through it, passing over paperwork, the stuff Sean had sent over relating to the properties abroad that Tom had signed up to. He had no idea what was happening with the other business ventures nor did he wish to know. The amount of paperwork was astonishing and Charles had a heap of other files as well tucked away in his briefcase concerning the safer investments Tom had made under his guidance.

It soon became apparent that the bulk of the money lost in Spain was irretrievable. Charles had to his credit, and well beyond the call of duty, spoken to Sean and in turn with whomever they could muster from the dodgy building firm and the local authority over there and it was clear that they had to rule a line through it. Trying to squeeze something out of it would ultimately fail and, worse, would cost them money in legal fees. The bottom line was they ought never to have signed the contract and the initial planning permission ought never to have been granted. Somebody somewhere had slipped up badly but just who that might be would be a difficult and ultimately impossible task to discover as they closed ranks.

Charles drew a sharp disbelieving breath as

Tom outlined what he had done already, how much money he had wasted in a vain last ditch attempt to make it work. He was not entirely sure although it would not surprise him in the least if Sean had actually tried bribing all and sundry, but he wanted nothing to do with that. He watched as he saw Charles taking his slim pen, crossing things out, doing quick sums in the margins, all the while shaking his head in bewilderment.

'Don't say it,' Tom said, when they had finished the post-mortem. He felt every bit as drained as if he had performed an actual one as the sizzle of excitement he had once felt turned into pure anxiety in his veins. For a while, for these last few years, it had been money not blood coursing through him and he now felt sick with the effort. 'I know I've cocked up. And it's no use blaming Sean completely.'

'You would have a good case. The man has clearly taken advantage of your naïvety.' Charles took off his half-moon reading spectacles and rubbed his eyes.

Tom frowned for no man likes to be accused of being naïve but he was big enough to acknowledge that it was not far from the truth. He had stupidly allowed Sean to bamboozle him with dazzling facts and figures and been wooed at the prospect of the beautiful villas on the hill. There was a real sense of disappointment that the completed ones, which did indeed look beautiful, would soon be gone, the vision crumbling in a heap of stones. What a complete and utter waste.

'The position is this.' Charles leaned forward and looked at him intently, the smallest of smiles flitting across his face. 'Don't look so worried. You don't need to sleep rough, not yet, but your fortune is severely depleted. I don't need to tell you that you've lost a huge amount of money. We must keep the remaining stocks that you have for a rainy day, for the pension fund, but you've sold off far too many shares when you should have held onto them and I don't need to tell you that there will have to be some changes made. You may own this house outright but you have considerable running costs, not to mention the staff,' he said, lowering his voice in case Annie — or was it Audrey? — was eavesdropping at the door. 'How many people do you employ?'

'Only four,' he said defensively. 'And I need my driver because I lost my licence last year.'

'You have your wife. She drives, doesn't she?' He paused until Tom acknowledged that. 'Well then. You have ceased your association with Mr . . . ' He checked the paperwork.

232

'You mean Sean?'

'Yes and not before time might I add, so you have no need for any further business trips to Preston or Spain, Mr Ross. Your wife can drive you around until your driving ban ceases. If you want to stay here then you will have to make changes. I can filter off a monthly income from the investments, sufficient to allow you to live comfortably. And you may wish to get yourself a job.' His smile was tight and unforgiving. 'It's not the end of the world, Tom. You are still a rich man.'

He noted the *Tom*.

'Once upon a time,' Charles said, as Tom showed him out, 'one million was perfectly sufficient to enjoy a lifetime of leisure and considerable luxury but now ten million is scarcely enough. But that's the way of the world.'

Quietly, Tom closed the door behind him.

At least, as Charles had said, the trust funds could not be touched for Melanie and Louisa and on top of that they still had Angela's money as a back up. As his wife had not been present they had not been able to go through her personal account but he was confident that Angela would still have the bulk of it left.

* * *

Barbara and Angela had lunched at The Turret and were taking a stroll together although Barbara's shockingly high heels prohibited a trek. They took a moment to sit on a bench by the railings of the promenade. There had been an overnight shower and the air felt sweet and fresh and there was the usual breeze from the bay, gleaming and silvery now, the sands empty aside from a few dog walkers.

Over lunch they had talked largely about Melanie. Angela was keeping quiet, yet, about the money situation and, although tempted by Barbara's concern, she had made no mention of that or of Cheryl and the intended visit she and Moira were shortly to make. She was already regretting telling Moira about Cheryl because she could surely continue to send money for she was probably reliant on the monthly gift and it would make things doubly hard for her if that money was suddenly whipped from under her feet. She refused to believe they were suddenly going to be stripped of everything and suspected Tom of over-reacting to what was a minor set-back.

'I told you before that you ought to shunt Melanie off somewhere to do some voluntary work,' Barbara said. 'You're far too soft with her.'

'I know that, but when I think of what could have happened it makes me think. When she fell down those steps, she could have been seriously hurt, Barbara, or even killed.' She drew a sharp breath for that thought was haunting her.

'But she wasn't. She's been a lucky girl.'

'We should never have taken her with us. It was doomed from the start although the girls seemed genuinely pleased to see each other at first and Melanie was much more her old self. She bought Louisa a lovely handbag out of her own money, a nice one from a department store but not ridiculously expensive. She didn't out-do the rest of us.'

'It's a start. It shows that she doesn't think only of herself. Maybe you dwell too much on the negative side. We all have our faults after all.'

'I'm only trying to do what's best for her. She just takes it all for granted. For instance I know that she would have kicked up an almighty fuss if Tom had not turned up trumps with her car. If he'd just bought her a little run-around which is what I wanted him to do she would have thrown the keys back in his face.'

'Is she still seeing this boy she met over there?'

Angela nodded. 'There are endless texts

235

and phone calls back and forth and he's coming over next weekend when I'm away.'

'Is that wise?'

'I don't know. I'm trying to keep calm, but it's going to cause endless trouble if it turns serious. If they get married for instance . . . '

'That's not very likely.'

'She's eighteen. I was that age when I met Tom and I knew exactly what I wanted then so she is old enough to know her own mind, but I want her to get a job and earn her living before she comes into her money. I want her to know what it's like to be out there working and I have to ask the question about Terry. Is he after her money?'

'You will always ask that question about any boy she goes with. You have to stop worrying. As you say, she's eighteen and it is time she started taking responsibility for her actions. I was running a business when I was eighteen. As for getting married, well, that's way into the future and I certainly can't see her sneaking off to do it. Knowing Melanie, she will want the full works and a bit more and she will expect dear daddy to foot the bill for it.'

Angela glanced sharply at her sensing that Barbara was becoming impatient with her and her inability to sort this out, but it was easy for her, a single lady, to talk.

The fact was Melanie's accusation levelled at her cousin had jolted her but she could not bring herself to talk to anybody about it, not even Tom. It was just way too serious. Melanie had said nothing more and she was hoping that time would heal and that providing she kept the two cousins apart for a while that silly accusation, probably a figment of her imagination in any case, would fade away.

But a little niggle remained. She had thought she always knew when Melanie was being honest for that little flick of her hair, the sideways look, was the giveaway when she was lying. And that night, in Moira's house, her gaze had been direct and open. What if it wasn't a figment of her imagination then, what if Louisa had really pushed her? What if the outcome had turned nasty and Melanie had been seriously injured, permanently damaged, or even dead? What then? They would never have known, that's what, and Louisa would have got away with murder. She thought about Louisa and the panicked look on her face that night. Did that signify guilt? Was it just a spur of the minute thing or had she been thinking about it all that evening and seized the opportunity as they passed by the head of those stairs? It would only take a nudge and Melanie's daft killer heels would see to the rest. That would make it premeditated and once upon a time you could have hanged for it.

Thinking that made her let out a gasp of horror.

'Snap out of it,' Barbara said, with an impatient click of her tongue. 'Oh the joy of darling daughters. I thank my lucky stars every day that I never had one.'

Angela made no comment, still deep in thought. She might ask Cheryl what she thought. She could talk to her about it because she could talk to her about *anything* and she could trust her not to discuss it with anyone although she was not supposed to be corresponding with her any more, not until she and Moira had seen her to explain the situation.

The sun broke through and Barbara, already wearing sunglasses, slipped off her cardigan jacket to reveal a low necked blouse, a diamond pendant nestled between her breasts. 'I love it here,' she said happily. 'When the sun shines it is just perfect. Just close your eyes and smell the sea and the sand.'

'And the seaweed? Look at it, it's everywhere.'

They laughed, got up and carried on walking.

'Have you ever walked across the sands, Angela?'

'You mean with the guide? No thanks.'

'You should. It scared me to death but he knows what he's doing. You have to put your trust in him. It's a fascinating experience.'

'I don't fancy being sucked down into quicksand.' She shivered despite the sun.

'Neither did I, but that won't happen with the guide. He knows these sands like the back of his hand. The trouble with you, Angela, is that you like to play it safe and after a while it's boring. There are times when you should go for it and sod the consequences.'

'I have a child,' Angela told her quietly. 'And it makes a big difference.'

'Touché.' Barbara shrugged. 'Let me know what happens with Melanie.' She glanced at her with a touch of exasperation. 'Moving on, darling. I've been thinking and I've come up with an idea. How do you fancy coming in with me and investing in a B&B with a difference?'

'I'm not sure. I need to think about it.' Angela could hardly contemplate such a thing just now, not when she and Tom were destined to have a *talk* this evening about their finances. She knew he was seeing Charles Grey at this very minute because he had asked if she wanted to be there. She had declined because she couldn't stand Charles the man even if Charles the financial adviser was the only person who might get them back on track. His expertise, however, could not hide the fact that he was reptilian and had a way of looking her up and down that made her skin crawl.

They should not panic because they were hardly going to be back where they started. They were not moving back to Woodland with their tails between their legs. They owed not a penny on the house so there was no reason they could not stay here although perhaps they might have to reduce the staff.

She laughed aloud at that and Barbara picked her up on it although she misunderstood the reason for it.

'What's so funny? This is not a common or garden B&B, darling. It's high on the hill and the views are superb. It has the potential to be top grade and for that you can ask over a hundred and fifty pounds per room per night. With my experience and your backing we could really make a go of it. I can turn out an excellent breakfast and you can organize that florist of yours to provide flowers throughout. Believe me it is little touches like that that matter. Success or failure treads a fine line but I know what I am talking about and I wouldn't be recommending it if it wasn't a sure thing. The woman who is selling it is utterly hopeless with no marketing skills whatsoever so it's no surprise she runs at a loss.'

'Sounds marvellous. How much is it selling for?'

Something had ignited in her as Barbara was talking. Barbara was keen and her enthusiasm was catching. She needed a project, something challenging and it would be good to have someone like Barbara to help. Together they could do the lot and Tom could do any painting and decorating. As for the interior, well, she did not need somebody like Megan to tell her what looked good.

And the most important thing of all was that at last she would be busy again.

'A quarter of a million,' Barbara was saying. 'Plus another hundred thousand possibly to do it up. It's a complete wreck but that's what is so wonderful about it. It's a blank canvas and I have big ideas.'

'I thought you had retired.' Angela glanced at her. 'It doesn't sound like it.'

'I did retire but I'm bored out of my mind. How old do you think I am?'

What an impossible question and not one she would like to get wrong.

'Old enough, let's say,' Barbara continued, smiling and saving her from an embarrassed guess. 'Take it from me, this is too good an opportunity to miss.'

Sean had said much the same thing to Tom but Sean was Sean and Barbara was astute and professional to the core.

'All right. I'll come and see it when I get back from Bath but I'm not making any promises.'

'You won't regret it. I'll tell the estate agent to inform the vendors that we are expressing serious interest. I know him and he won't sell it to anybody else in the meantime.'

Angela sighed. When had she said she was *seriously* interested? The trouble with Barbara was that, once she got an idea in her head, it took some shifting.

★　★　★

The reply to the last letter was late.

Returning from the Maldives, relaxed after a week spent doing nothing except lie in the sun and swim in the ocean, it was a surprise and disappointment to see there was no padded envelope propped on the sideboard in Uncle Walter's sitting-room.

'No, it hasn't come yet,' Uncle Walter said, anticipating the question. 'And don't look at me like that. It's not my fault.' His glance was critical. 'You look like you've been in the sun.

You want to watch that. It can give you cancer for somebody fair skinned like you. What was it like then, the Maldives?'

'Lovely, thanks.'

'I see you've been to the supermarket.' He took in the three or four Sainsbury bags dumped in the hall. 'Does that mean you're going to make my tea?'

'Dead right. I've got some quick fry steaks, onion rings, a bag of chips and your favourite tin of mushy peas. I thought we might have a nice meal together for a change.'

'What's for pudding?'

'Blackcurrant pie.'

'Homemade?' He laughed heartily. 'Only kidding.'

It was a bit of a worry wondering why the parcel was late because Angela made sure the reply always came before the end of the month, writing her reply on virtually the same day each month — the 15th — but there might be a perfectly reasonable explanation. Thinking about it, the last letter to Angela had maybe been a little over the top and perhaps Cheryl should stop laying it on quite so thick because Angela was an intelligent woman and it would not take much for her to start having doubts although, strangely enough, most of what Cheryl had written was true, information gleaned from the unfortunate Paula. She was a pain in the arse these days and it was not much fun being the shoulder she was crying onto. Sooner or later she would have to be given the push as she was becoming clingy.

Sitting at the kitchen table tucking into their steak and chips with Uncle Walter in a happy mood it was easy to drop in the request for him to phone as soon as the parcel arrived.

'Can I phone you at work? Or will that boss of yours not like that?'

'It's OK. He won't mind. Ring me on my mobile.'

'You have to be careful sending a lot of cash through the post,' Uncle Walter said, waving his knife about, a sharp knife coated in tomato sauce so that the gesture looked even more menacing. 'You should tell whoever sends it that it's asking for trouble. It will get intercepted one of these days.'

'Intercepted? Don't be daft. And there's been no problem with the cash, not in five years.'

'I *knew* it.' He put the knife down, grinned. 'I knew you were blackmailing somebody, you little sod. There is no Cheryl Fisher, is there? It's you. You're pretending to be her and don't deny it.'

'It's not blackmail. I'm doing this woman a service, Uncle Walt. She needs to write to

Cheryl and there's no harm in that.'

'Tell that to the marines. I'll say this for you, Colin, you are a chip off the old block, but I want you to know that I won't grass on you because you've done more for me than that dad of yours ever did. Tell me now, how much is she sending you because I reckon I'm owed a percentage for keeping my mouth shut?'

17

The country house hotel was impressive, straight out of a television period drama, a Palladian mansion set in thirty acres of parkland.

It was a long drive and Angela refused to let her take the wheel so they had plenty of loo and coffee stops on the way but they breathed a sigh of relief as Angela finally drew the car to a halt and a porter swiftly appeared to take their bags. Moira had bought some new outfits for the weekend determined not to be outdone by her sister's effortlessly classy wardrobe. They were in one of the grandest rooms, a room on the first floor with extensive views of the terrace and golf course beyond. The ensuite was a blue tiled heaven and there were complimentary bath-robes and the biggest fluffiest towels you have ever seen.

Their bags were carried up to their room and Angela gave the porter a generous tip before kicking off her shoes and lying on top of the beautiful bedspread. 'I'm bagging this one,' she said with a pleased sigh.

The first thing Moira did was put the kettle

on and get the cups out of the cupboard, the milk out of the little fridge, ruing inwardly that she just could not shake off her domestic streak. She brewed them a pot of tea and opened the little packet of shortbread biscuits, Angela sitting back and letting her do the lot.

'I still can't get over being able to afford something like this,' Angela said, taking her tea through to the balcony. 'Isn't it fabulous?'

'Crazy,' Moira agreed, childishly thrilled by the splendour of their suite where they would occupy twin beds just as if they were youngsters again, chatting quietly to each other long after lights out. Their room at their childhood home in Woodland had suffered a little from their mother's over-elaborate styling although they had not noticed so much then. The colour scheme changed little over the years, pink and pretty with matching girly duvet covers, but when they were fifteen and fourteen respectively Dilys got their dad to finally clear the junk room so that they could have the separate rooms they craved.

It had been fantastic to have a room of her own, but privately Moira missed Angela and wondered if she in turn missed her.

It would be nice to be close together again and Moira said as much, wondering why they had not thought to do this before, to have a weekend away together, just the two of them without the men so that they could well and truly relax. There was something on her mind, however, but she wanted to settle in before she broached the subject of Melanie and Louisa.

Angela did it for her.

'How is Louisa these days?' she asked. 'Is she still upset about Melanie's accident?'

'She's fine,' Moira said carefully. 'What about Mel?'

'She's fine physically,' Angela told her. 'But I worry about her because I can't get through to her. She needs to work but whenever I bring it up she goes all huffy on me and says I'm nagging her. Whoever heard of an eighteen year old who is not interested in getting a job? She just slouches around the house all day. You'd think money grows on trees the way she spends it. I know . . . ' — she lifted up a hand resignedly — 'I know, we've made her like it.'

'Could she not get onto a course at college?'

Angela made a face. 'With her results? You must be joking. I did suggest a re-sit but she wouldn't hear of it.'

'OK.' Moira raised a hand in apology. 'I agree that she should get a job but the problem is she doesn't need one.'

'Exactly. It's a terrible position to be in.'

'Have you tried being blunt and just telling her straight that she has to get off her arse and do something?'

'More or less, but she storms off as soon as I start laying down the law and Tom's no help whatsoever. For him, she can do no wrong. What happened to her, Moira? Was it the money or the school?'

'A bit of both I should think. If I remember Adele had a rebellious streak around that age. Do you remember that boyfriend Jon?'

Angela laughed. 'I do. You were really panicking then, weren't you?'

'She only did it to annoy me.' Moira smiled. 'So maybe you shouldn't make too much of this. I would just back off for a while and let her think about it. She'll get over it.'

'I hope so. Thanks for reminding me about Adele. I had forgotten.'

'They all go through it although, thank God, Louisa has her feet firmly on the ground.' She hesitated before asking. 'Is Mel still going out with Terry?'

'He was supposed to be coming over to see her this weekend but just before I set out she tells me it's off. She texted him, apparently.' She pulled a face. 'Isn't that awful? You should always tell somebody news like that face to face.'

Quite.

'So it's all over. That didn't last long,' Moira said tightly.

'No, she sent him packing pretty quickly and I feel badly about that because of Louisa. I don't know what Melanie was thinking of. Allowing him to be all over her at the party was unforgivable. I tried to warn her but short of creating a scene I could do nothing.'

'Same here.'

'I am so sorry, Moira. I can't believe she was so insensitive.'

'It's all right. Lou will get over it. If Terry could do something like that then he wasn't worth the hassle. She's going to be very busy from now on so it's just as well. I think she felt it though. She imagined herself to be in love and you know what it's like and how that first rejection feels like the end of the world.'

'It's hard.' Angela had the grace to flush, probably remembering of what she, too, was guilty.

'She's a tough nut. I knew it was going to end in tears but we can't dictate who our girls get involved with, can we? That's the worst thing we can do and I'm only just realizing it. The all-time great scenario I dream about is for Louisa to meet another medical student and fall in love and get married later on when they're qualified. But that probably won't happen.'

'Who can tell? They're grown ups although Melanie doesn't always act like one. She doesn't give people a chance, gets bored far too easily and ditches them. I think she worries that they are only going out with her because of the money. She's never broken-hearted so I assume *she* always ends it. She just plays with them. I worry that one day she's going to get really hurt when the same thing happens to her. When *she* falls in love and it isn't returned.'

For a few moments they were silent, the silence broken by the sound of a golf club cleanly striking a ball and a few shouts of laughter.

'Louisa seems upset by the accident.' Moira stretched out her legs, shading her eyes from the sun and watching the little chatty group congregating on the first tee. 'I think she blames herself for it. She was very concerned about tearing the dress, even asked me if she should offer to get Melanie a new one.'

'I thought it was Leo who tore the dress. Anyway, it doesn't matter. She says she wasn't that keen on it anyway because although it cost a lot it looked like something she could have got in Dorothy Perkins.'

Moira raised her eyebrows. She still shopped there, sometimes. But Melanie was Melanie and used to the good life. How would *her* girls have reacted if they had won the money? Remembering how Adele had used her gift to buy her flat spending scarcely any of it on herself, she wondered. As for Jim, well, he might have favoured a move to a bigger house but it would still be in Woodland and it would have been something that needed doing up to keep him occupied. One thing was sure: they wouldn't have lost money as Tom had, although, to be honest, she rather admired the cavalier approach which reflected Tom's style. Anyone who could let a few million pounds slip through his fingers had to be cautiously admired.

'I hope you won't mind me saying it, Angie, but I think Melanie's turned into a snob of the worst kind and you encourage it. You should never have bought her that car for her birthday. What were you thinking of?'

'It was Tom's idea. I've told you I want to shame her into getting a job. She wouldn't apply for a thing if I didn't make notes of job vacancies and present them to her on a plate. Sometimes I've even written out her CV for her, made it sound better than it is, hoping that she'll show some interest at the interview. She looks good, doesn't she, and they taught her to speak well so on paper it always seems promising. She usually gets to the interview stage so I think they give her the benefit of the doubt.' She snatched a glance at Moira. 'I don't suppose you could talk some sense into her. She takes notice of what you say.'

'I could try the sympathetic aunt approach, but I might end up shaking her.'

They sighed, the Melanie problem casting a cloud over their previous good humour. The forecast today was mainly cloudy with some sunny spells, good enough for a round of golf although the players on the first tee were suffering a painfully bad start, their laughter carrying on the breeze.

Idly, Moira picked up the hotel folder and leafed through it.

'Shall we book a facial and things?' she asked.

'Of course. We'll do the lot. Manicure, pedicure, massage, whatever you fancy. You can go swimming and I'll do something else then. We can do it this afternoon.'

'Don't forget Adele's joining us for dinner.'

'Will she be bringing Michael along?'

'I think so unless he's on duty. They work shifts so I don't know how they work out their lives together. They seem to be ships that pass in the night. God alone knows how they sort out their sex life.'

Angela raised her eyebrows but made no comment.

'Mum keeps on about them getting married, but Adele's not the least maternal,' Moira went on. 'She's already said I've not to hold my breath for grandchildren so what's the point in them risking spoiling things by getting married when they're perfectly happy as they are? He's good for her, Angie, and he told her from the start he wasn't interested in the money and I don't think he is.'

'Fair enough. Mum has a cheek to keep going on about them getting married. Her own wasn't that good, was it? She led poor Dad a merry dance. All she thought about was the business,' she said with a bitterness that surprised Moira. 'What did she ever do for us?'

'Oh come on, she did her best. It can't have been easy for her.'

'I suppose not.'

'You were the favourite,' Moira said, feeling the sun prickle on her face. 'Still are. She's always on about you, Angie, and what you're up to. You could never have kept it a secret when you won the money even if you had wanted to.'

'She was always one for favourites,' Angela smiled a little. 'It's obvious for instance that

Louisa is the favourite granddaughter.'

'Only because she's the youngest.'

'Just. She's only a few months younger than Melanie. She's such a good girl, Mother keeps telling me, buckles down to her work, gets fantastic grades, and helps round the house without a word of complaint. The saintly Louisa, no less.'

Moira glanced at her sharply, bristling at what sounded suspiciously like sarcasm. 'Like it or not, it's true. She is a good girl, always has been. She's never given me a minute's trouble since she was born. She slept through the night right from the start.'

'Don't rub it in. You know Melanie was a nightmare.'

'We were just lucky and, don't forget, she was double the birth-weight of Melanie.'

'And it's stayed that way.'

Moira bit her lip. Bloody hell; it didn't matter what Angela said she was not going to be drawn into reacting.

'I'm proud of her, Angie.'

'And I'm not proud of *my* daughter?'

She shrugged. 'You tell me.'

The atmosphere was going sour, the sun retreating behind a cloud as if to emphasize that so that the temperature plummeted. Oh come on, they weren't going to spoil the weekend, were they, by starting to act like

Tom and Jim? They were big girls and they should rise above it.

'Maybe your Louisa isn't such a good girl after all,' Angela said softly. She rarely lost her temper, but sometimes the quiet snarls she had been known to utter were worse and much more menacing than outright yelling.

'What do you mean?'

Oh for goodness sake, this was going from bad to worse and they were due to spend the whole weekend together. They should put a stop to this before it went any further, but she couldn't allow Angela to make such a statement without substantiating it.

What the hell was she getting at?

'I have talked to Melanie and she's told me something that has really upset me, Moira. I was going to keep quiet, but I don't know that I should. I've been put into an impossible position and I can't win either way. If I say it, you're going to be annoyed and if I don't say it, it's as if I don't believe my own daughter.'

'For Christ's sake, Angela, if you've got something to say, spit it out. I can't be doing with all this mystery.'

'For the sake of the family,' Angela went on, sounding suddenly very much like their mother in one of her grand moods. 'Melanie and I agreed we are not going to take it any further and I have not mentioned this to Tom or anybody else.'

'Not even Cheryl?'

'No. You know I haven't written lately now that we are going to see her. She'll be wondering what's going on. I don't think I would have told her anyway; I thought about it but it would be just too risky. This has to kept *en famille*.'

Moira frowned and sat up straighter. 'Please tell me, Angie. You're worrying me now.'

'I'm sorry to say this to you, but according to Melanie it was no accident. The fact is Louisa pushed her down those stairs.'

'And you believe that?' Even as she laughed, Moira felt her maternal hackles rising. 'You believe what your spoilt little rich kid says when it's obvious she's just plain jealous of Louisa and what she's going to do with her life. Louisa's going to be a doctor and the way she's going Melanie will be damned lucky to get a job in McDonald's. For all her expensive education — '

'That's right. Bring that up.'

'Well it's true. There's no denying it, is there? Maybe if Tom hadn't had such big ideas it would have turned out differently.' She waved a dismissive hand. 'Good God, isn't it enough that she nicked Lou's

257

boyfriend? I'm not saying it would have lasted, but that's not the bloody point, is it?'

'There's no need to swear or to raise your voice either.' Angela stood up. 'Voices carry out here. If we're going to argue let's do it inside please. We don't need an audience.'

Somebody had appeared on another balcony a little way away giving them a cheery wave.

Muttering, Moira got up and followed her inside, sliding the door shut. She could not believe what she was hearing. If Melanie dared repeat that accusation to anybody, and someone in authority got wind of it, it could lead to a whole lot of trouble. Rumours could escalate and it could ruin Louisa's career if the college heard. My goodness, she had it in for her and no mistake and all because Melanie had failed her exams so spectacularly that it had been an embarrassment for the school which generally turned out mature, balanced young women.

'Right. Let's have it again,' Moira said, standing with her arms folded. She was determined to have it out; to wipe the floor with Angela if necessary for there was absolutely no way that there was any truth in this.

In the time it took to come inside the room, the fight had gone out of Angela and she sank down onto one of the beds, head in hands.

Moira waited at a distance. She was disturbed that there would not be a full-blown, get-it-out-in-the-open row. The trouble with her sister was that she had no fight in her, would buckle and deflate in an instant directly somebody stood up to her.

'I'm sorry.' After a moment, she looked up, pushing her hair out of her face, a face now damp with tears. 'I'm only telling you what Melanie said. Oh Moira, why would she say such an awful thing if it wasn't true? I can't believe she would lie about something like that. I was so pleased because the two of them seemed to be getting on so well together. It was just like old times for a while.'

'Don't start crying, for goodness sake. That won't help.' Moira knew it was best not to offer too much sympathy. She reached for a pack of tissues on the dressing-table top and passed them over so that Angela could give her nose a good blow. 'I'll speak to Louisa but I'll have to do it carefully. I'll just ask her what happened exactly and we'll take it from there.'

'Thanks. I could kill her sometimes.'

Moira tried a smile as Angela reached for another tissue. 'I hope you're talking about Melanie,' she said.

Nothing more was said and Angela regretted saying anything in the first place. Why could she not keep quiet about things where her sister was concerned? She wished she had not mentioned Cheryl now because Moira was quite determined that all would be resolved this weekend when they paid the surprise visit to her. Angela had bought a parting gift, something pretty and feminine as a little treat, and she would write a hefty final cheque as well just to assuage her conscience. She was just hoping that actually meeting her face to face would not prove to be a dreadful mistake and just make things more awkward than they already were. There was still time to back out, but Moira was up for it and would take some persuading when her mind was made up.

They were soothed by the treatments in the beauty salon and afterwards whilst Moira went for a dip in the pool, Angela sat in the hotel lounge and ordered tea and cake. Tonight she was going to try to forget about the problems with Melanie and Tom and just enjoy dinner with Adele, her favourite niece. It was unfair to have favourites but in their family it seemed par for the course. She admired Adele's fighting spirit, the little shots of temper, the cuteness when she was little, the way she always came to her aunty for a cuddle and the total lack of jealousy when, having been an only child for eight long years, baby Louisa had arrived on the scene.

Living as close as they did to each other in the early days, it was hardly surprising that Adele became Melanie's big sister, too, in a way and it occurred to her that perhaps if anybody could talk sense into her daughter it might be Adele.

18

The street took some finding. It was not the prettiest of neighbourhoods and at the top of the street there was a pub, shuttered and forbidding, and opposite that a former church that was now a tile and bathroom centre.

'My stomach's churning,' Angela said, pulling on the handbrake and peering over the road. She had stopped a few doors away, the car attracting the glances of a group of youths who were hanging about. The house was in the middle of a terrace of Victorian houses, many of them already converted into flats and student accommodation which was, of course, the kiss of death. 'I should have phoned her first. You can't just turn up on somebody's doorstep.'

Moira glanced sharply at her. 'Do you have her phone number?'

'No but I could have found out, couldn't I?'

'She might be ex-directory.'

'Why?'

'Because of the bother with the ex and all that.'

'I didn't think of that. We are ex-directory too, of course.'

'*Of course*. To stop all the begging calls,' Moira said with a wry smile. 'Haven't you ever asked for her number? In case you needed to contact her urgently?'

'I didn't see the point. We said right at the beginning that this was just a postal thing. We were never going to meet or phone each other and we've stuck to it.'

'You're crackers, the pair of you. After all this time I would have been dying to find out what she looks like. There's something funny about all this, Angie. It doesn't add up. I don't like it.'

They were in no rush to leave the safety of the car and it seemed from Moira's expression that she shared Angela's misgivings. There was a distinct air of menace, this particular street having long given up any attempts to beautify it. Saplings that had been planted here and there were struggling to survive, composted with a build up of litter and cans and dog dirt. It was heartbreaking to think of Cheryl, a vulnerable unhappy woman, having to survive in this environment. Angela realized that the woman's attempt to talk about her home with pride was sheer bravado. Quite obviously she hadn't wanted Angela to know the truth, that it looked as bad as this.

Number 116 was not the worst in the row, that dubious accolade surely going to next door where a rusty old motor bike was languishing in the front garden as well as an upturned supermarket trolley, although oddly there was an enormous satellite dish on the wall which looked capable of receiving pictures from Mars. As for Cheryl's garden that was a shock because she had seemed to be every bit as interested in gardening as Angela. The garden at No. 116 was dreadful, hugely overgrown with an ancient apple tree overhanging the wall causing passers-by to duck under the branches.

'What if she's not in?' she asked Moira as they sat quietly, uncertain but safe in what felt like an armoured vehicle as the youths accompanied by a vicious-looking bull terrier shot fitful glances their way. 'I can't just spring this on her. This was a mad idea just coming out of the blue and expecting her to be in.'

'I thought you told me she doesn't get out much.'

'True.' She knew all about Cheryl's daily routine. She had tried a few part-time jobs to fit round the school day but the holidays had proved a trial because she could not leave Richard. It was the holidays now so maybe the routine was a bit different although she knew that Cheryl never had a holiday as such. She had once considered paying for one, surprising her, but she knew how wary Cheryl was of taking Richard away from the things he was familiar with.

'We're here now anyway,' Moira said. 'And the longer we sit here the worse it will be. Come on, let's stop being wimps and go and ring the bell.'

'I don't like the look of those boys. What if they damage the car? They could scratch the paintwork or let the tyres down or something.'

'You are paranoid.' Moira drew in a sharp breath. 'I know they look like they'd slit your throat as soon as look at you, but they're just kids and we are mothers. It's just a matter of choosing the right words. Just look at them, they need to pull up their trousers and tie their laces.' There was a brief pause as the biggest boy in the group, a mean-looking individual with a slicked back hairstyle, looked directly at them vainly hitching up his baggy jeans as if he had heard what Moira had said. With a world weary motherly sigh, Moira contemplated his cocky demeanour, wondering what angle to take. Would firm and friendly do the trick, or should she be more aggressive? Not being a mother of sons felt like a distinct disadvantage just now.

'Or alternatively I could just bribe them to look after the car for us,' Angela suggested with a rare show of street cred.

'Brilliant. Wish I'd thought of that.'

'How much?' Angela delved into her bag and produced her purse rifling through the notes.

'Give them a tenner to start with and if the car's in one piece when we get back they get a further twenty. That should do it.'

'Thirty pounds? It doesn't seem a lot.'

'Believe me, Angie, to them it will be a small fortune.'

★   ★   ★

The gate was half hanging off its hinges and Moira stepped in something on the way up the path, cursing softly and wiping the heel of her shoe on the edge of the lawn or what passed for it. The house had an empty look to it, the curtains at the grimy window having seen better days, drawn apart to reveal a gloomy interior.

'It's a dump,' Moira whispered.

'I know. I didn't expect it to be like this,' Angela said, trying in vain to equate this dingy property with the home Cheryl wrote about so lovingly. What had happened to the flowery curtains she had made herself, grabbing some bargain material in the market and doing the lot on an old sewing machine?

There was a long wait before the door-bell was answered but, just as they were about to give up, they could hear feet shuffling towards the door.

At last, there was the sound of many bolts being drawn back by somebody who clearly took security seriously and the door swung open to reveal an old man wearing a grey cardigan, his attempts to shave this morning resulting in an interesting collection of toilet paper stuck to blobs of blood on his face.

'*What?*' he asked aggressively. 'If you're from the council you can forget it. I've paid that bloody bill so you haven't a leg to stand on if you're here to complain. You should stick to your side of the deal and empty those bins that have been sitting there stinking for over a week now. We'll have rats before you know it and if I get one of those bastards in my kitchen I'm suing you.'

Big sister Moira took charge.

'We're not from the council,' she said with a smile. 'Is Cheryl in?'

'Cheryl?' Instantly his face changed, slyness replacing the anger and it was almost as if they could see his brain ticking over as the silence lengthened. A radio was on and they could hear the sound of laughter. Angela was just about to repeat the question when he spoke with eyes averted. 'No. She isn't. She's out.'

'Where? What time will she be back?'

'How the hell would I know?'

'Are you Uncle Charlie?' Angela ventured, recalling the complicated family tree. 'Are you visiting Cheryl just now?'

'Visiting?' He was holding firmly onto the door, not inviting them in but staring at them, eyes now flickering uneasily from one to the other. They were dressed down for the occasion, jeans and T-shirts but, clean and well-groomed, they still stood out in this street like models on a catwalk. 'Might be,' he said at last with a shrug of his shoulders. 'What do you want?'

'Is Richard here?' Angela asked, although of course the likelihood of him being left in this man's charge was laughable.

'Richard?' Doubts fluttered over his face. 'Look, Cheryl isn't in and I don't know when he . . . she . . . will be back so sorry I can't help.'

'Will you ask her to ring me?' Angela said, desperate now as she saw that the end of this conversation was in sight. 'Tell her it's Angela. This is my number.' She thrust a scrap of paper at him. 'It's urgent.'

The door shut in their faces.

★ ★ ★

'How can I ring her? I'm supposed to be Cheryl,' Colin said, taking in the news of the visit and finding that he was not entirely surprised. Giving out a real address always had a risk attached but he didn't see how it could operate otherwise. The letters had to go somewhere and he needed to be one step back. In any case, his address had an upbeat sound to it, executive properties in a former dockside area that was now the hub of a restaurant and upmarket club culture, apartments built for singles with money. It had been a good run and well done to Uncle Walter for not giving the game away although as he said he had nearly slipped up.

'That Angela's a bonny-looking woman,' Uncle Walt said. 'They looked a bit alike but the other one was fatter and her hair was too short. Hard-faced I reckon. She didn't say much.'

'It would have been her sister Moira,' Colin said, thinking hard. So Angela had traced him to this address, which was no secret, but with Uncle Walter in on it it would be a dead end for her if she returned. He could write a quick letter now, this minute, with some sob story about how the two of them — Cheryl and Richard — had been forced to leave the

269

address and that he had had to leave Uncle Charlie in charge of sorting stuff out. He needed a new address for her letters to go to but he had mates whom he could bribe to save his mail for him.

He reached for his car keys, anxious now to be off. He had to pitch the next letter exactly right so he would have to use all his creative talents. He would have to take a risk and say thank you and goodbye but with a bit of luck and a following wind she might just see her way to carrying on. Pity if it did end because that extra money coming his way each month made all the difference.

This had better be good.

★   ★   ★

There was no phone call but there was a letter a few days later.

The weekend had been a qualified success although it was annoying that nothing had been resolved as far as Cheryl was concerned. Moira had suggested returning the next day but Angela had said no. Maybe fate had stepped in and maybe she and Cheryl were destined never to meet. It occurred that for all the disappointment she had in an odd way been relieved too. She did not really want to see what Cheryl looked like in the flesh.

'Did you ever go to that WI? They seem to be writing to you again,' Melanie said, bringing the letters through.

'What WI?'

For a minute she could not remember what she had said but then that was the trouble with lying, it caught up with you. She picked up the letter and waited until Melanie was gone before she read it quickly.

There was a different address on the top.

My dear Angela

I didn't get your last letter but I wouldn't be surprised if Uncle Charlie has thrown it away. What a time I've had! It's been hell on earth and at one time I genuinely feared for our lives. Uncle Charlie's a lazy old so and so and seems to think that he can just drop in and have me look after him whenever he wants. He's done it before and he gets me so upset that I can't think straight. I didn't ask but I think he's just served a term and I didn't ask what it was for either. He's a terrible influence on Richard and even though I've told him time and time again he still doesn't know how to treat him. He keeps saying '*look at me, boy*' which is absolutely the wrong thing *to* say.

271

Anyway, he pushed in and said he was going to live with us for a while because he'd been booted out of his last place. I know that legally I could kick him out but I can't be bothered with all the fuss and I daren't risk upsetting him. He's evil, Angela, and he's a man you have to stay away from. If you ever met him you would see exactly what I mean.

He doesn't know where I am and it has to stay that way. I decided that the best thing we could do was for us to move away fast. To be honest it was a dump. I am sorry, Angela, but I was so ashamed of that last place I lived in that I made it sound a lot better than it was. I can tell you now that it was terrible living there but Richard was fond of his room and you know how difficult it is to talk about moving with him. I just bundled all his stuff in a big box and brought it here. Luckily I have this friend who gave us a lift otherwise I don't know what I would have done.

Richard is being difficult. He keeps asking when we are going home but I am hoping that he will settle down here because this place is so much nicer and I am going to make us a proper home, a nice home instead of that dump we were in before. You should have seen it, the neighbourhood was really dodgy and we kept getting broken into so there was no point in having nice things. I tried for a while, I really tried, but they trashed my lovely garden so I just gave up on it. It broke my heart seeing that garden go to seed and I couldn't bring myself to tell you about it.

Can you forgive me for lying to you? How could I tell you the truth that I am a useless mother who can't even find a nice home for her child? He is the only thing that matters to me and my heart aches for him because he does not understand that he has a new room now in a new home. He wants his old room, but I expect Uncle Charlie will have put somebody else in by now but that's the landlord's problem not mine. I have forfeited getting my deposit back by moving out although I don't owe any rent. I am paid up to date thanks to you.

I quite understand if you decide to stop writing to me and sending me money. I quite understand. Thank you very much for helping us out for the last five years. I am eternally grateful for that. I think of you as my fairy godmother. I have given you nothing and you have given me so much.

I hope your problems are sorted out soon and that Melanie gets a job.

Goodbye.

Love from Cheryl.

XXX

19

When Angela returned home, she spoke to Melanie touching on the thorny subject of Louisa. Had Melanie really said that Louisa had pushed her down those stairs? A bad fall and a bump to the head can do funny things to your memory and it had been very late at night in a strange bed in a strange room.

'Mum, I don't want to talk about that ever again,' Melanie told her. 'You shouldn't have said anything to Aunty Moira. It was supposed to be private between you and me. Please forget I ever said it. I was just tired and everything was aching and — '

'Then it *was* just the shock and the medication talking?' Angela said with relief.

After a moment, Melanie turned away but not before she gave an almost imperceptible nod of her head.

★   ★   ★

They were on their way to visit the potential B&B. Left to her own devices, Angela would have been happy to forget it but Barbara was insistent and in the end just to keep her happy she agreed to be shown round.

Barbara picked her up, wearing the tightest white jeans ever and the sort of heels that had been Melanie's downfall.

'A few words of advice, darling: don't say a lot,' she said. 'That way *they* have to keep talking. And don't enthuse about it at all. If you like it and if you think we can work with it then give me a signal like this . . . ' — she touched her nose and rubbed it. 'Try your best to look as if it's doing nothing for you at all.'

Angela laughed. 'I don't see why we can't say we like it. We won't be signing any paperwork, not straight off.'

'It's a game. If we want it for the best possible price then it's essential to play the not so keen approach.'

'If we like it then I'm not playing about with numbers,' Angela told her. 'It's only a quarter of a million so we can easily afford it.'

'Don't forget the cost of doing it up.' Barbara seemed exasperated. 'We should get it for just over two hundred thousand if we play our cards right. The less we spend, the more we have to play with.'

Only a quarter of a million. Had she really said that?

★　★　★

Moira sometimes used Louisa as an emergency fill-in as she was a good worker. It was just as well she had a back-up system because a lot of her cleaners were struck down just now with a summer bug which was causing Moira a headache.

It meant that she, as well as Louisa, had to roll up her sleeves today.

There were two adjacent holiday cottages to clean and they needed to get them in sparkling condition long before the two-o'clock deadline. Usually it was just a question of changing the linen followed by a quick tidy-up but sometimes you didn't know where to start.

'To think I was living a life of luxury last weekend with your Aunty Angela,' Moira called out, dragging the vacuum cleaner out of its cupboard.

'Knowing you, I bet you tidied up before you left.' Louisa's voice came from the bathroom where she was now cleaning the toilet.

'I would have but Angela said to leave it. She left two twenty pound notes for the housekeeping staff and we were only there for two nights.'

Louisa laughed. 'She's certainly learned how to live the good life.'

Moira switched on the vacuum cleaner and

for a while it was impossible to speak. When the carpets were clean, the linen changed and all surfaces wiped, she put the kettle on so that they could have a quick break before they tackled the cottage next door. Checking the time she saw they were well on target and maybe they could spend some time together later this afternoon. She paid Louisa the going rate for the cleaning hours she put in, but in addition she wanted to treat her to a few new bits and pieces to take to university. She would buy her a couple of pairs of jeans and some sweaters; nothing fancy, just casual stuff for her to wear to the lectures for she didn't want her daughter looking too scruffy and letting the side down.

She was so lucky to have such a good girl, she thought, peeping into the bathroom and seeing that it was now as clean as could be. Louisa was flushed from her efforts, surveying it with satisfaction. Knowing the state the previous occupants had left it in Moira patted her on the back and whispered a 'well done'.

They sat down in the kitchen with two mugs of strong coffee.

'So what did you and Aunty Angie get up to?'

'The usual stuff. We had massages and manicures and I had a swim and Adele came over for dinner on Friday night.'

'Yes, she texted me. Aunty Angie asked her to talk to Melanie.'

'She asked me, too, but we agreed in the end that Adele might be a better bet. I didn't like to land her in it but Angela is desperate for somebody to talk some sense into her. When I think what she used to be like I could weep.'

'Oh Mum, you have no idea, have you? She was never the sweet little thing you thought she was. The truth is she was never liked,' Louisa said. 'You have no idea what went on. Even before she went off to that school, I used to have to make excuses for her the whole time because she was family. She was uppity even then and she always thought she was better than us, and prettier, of course. She had a high-handed attitude that got up everybody's nose.'

'Did she now?' Moira could not help a little smile, thinking of Angela and the cotton-wool treatment she had always afforded her only precious daughter and how in the end it was so much better to do what she had done and let them breathe. Adele and Louisa were supreme examples of that and it was hard not to allow a little smugness to creep into her thoughts. 'I know it's been a difficult time for both of you, with that thing with Terry and everything . . .'

Louisa laughed. 'I've forgotten all about *him*. You could say she did me a favour because I'm going to make sure next time that I'm not taken in like that. Just because he's the first boy to take any notice of me I thought he was the love of my life. Isn't that mad? How do you know for sure if somebody's genuine, Mum? How do you know if they mean what they say?'

'You know.' She smiled.

'Did you know right away when you met Dad that he was your Mr Right?'

'I'd known him vaguely for years,' she said. 'So it wasn't exactly a spur of the minute thing. We just got to know each other gradually and we found that we had the same daft sense of humour. I realized how much I would miss him if he wasn't around. That's a good test I suppose.'

'You make it sound a bit ordinary. I thought it was all about sparks flying.'

'That's just the movies, love.'

But of course it was not.

Her thoughts drifted to Tom on the evening of Louisa's party sitting beside him on that sofa, the casual touch of his arm on her shoulder that caused a surge of longing to sweep through her, the way he had looked at her, what she had read into that look and the way she had very nearly shed her sisterly inhibitions and just kissed *him* and have done with it. She would have shown him what he was missing.

'I'm glad you're over all that then,' Moira picked up the mugs. 'And we should be grateful that Melanie's accident wasn't any worse. It could have been nasty. People can die from falling down steps like that.'

She was watching Louisa carefully. She knew her daughter. She could hear her voice on the phone and know instinctively by the tone of the voice if something was wrong. She remembered the panic in both her voice and her face on that evening; an understandable panic in view of what had happened but, in the car on the way to the hospital she recalled how Louisa had brushed her hand aside, how she had sat quietly alone with her thoughts. She remembered the gasp from her when that daft Leo was spouting on about the way a head injury can go wrong.

'Tell me something, love: did you push her down those stairs?' she asked, the question a mere whisper. 'You can tell me the truth, it won't go any further.'

Louisa, the good girl, *her* good girl, the girl who had given her so much joy, her princess no less, looked up, astonished. 'I can't believe you've asked me that, Mother,' she said. 'Did Melanie say I did?'

She nodded.

'The bitch. She's lying. It all happened so fast. I might have reached out to grab her, to try to stop her falling, but to say that I pushed her is just awful. We were passing the stairs and she was wearing those silly shoes and she kept hitching up her skirt because it was getting caught in the shoes. I was behind her and Terry was beside her and Leo was there and then the next minute, she tripped up and lost her balance and me and Leo grabbed at the dress and . . . ' Her eyes were suddenly blurry as the words tailed away. 'Mum, I can't believe you've asked me that.'

'It's OK.' Moira put up a hand. 'Don't get upset. She was just confused later and she should never have said it. Thank goodness she only told her mother. Aunty Angela won't tell anybody else. Let's just forget it.'

'Thanks Mum. You know I would never dream of doing something like that. I hope Aunty Angela didn't believe her.'

'Not for a minute. Come on, young lady. We have work to do.'

Following her out, Moira knew she had made one big mistake in asking the question for it really did not matter what Louisa said: Mothers always knew.

Angela was right. It would stay in the family. There was something to be said for keeping some things buttoned up.

Sometimes it is far better *not* to know.

★ ★ ★

It was on a hilly road with extensive views of the glorious sweep of the bay — great store was placed on that — and the agent's representative was waiting for them. They were late, by accident not design, but Angela saw the relief on the woman's face as she came forward to greet them, commenting favourably on Barbara's little car which was a good Brownie points earner.

'So nice to meet you, Mrs Delamere and Mrs Ross,' she gushed. 'I'm Caroline Chambers. Do come in. You've seen the brochure of course,' she added, as they followed her inside.

'You are probably aware that I have already been shown round by your colleague,' Barbara explained. 'I have to say I am put off by the amount of work that is needed, but Angela, my business partner, insisted on seeing it although we have one or two others in mind. Don't we, Angela?'

Angela, put on the spot, could only nod her agreement.

'Granted it is in need of some repair and renovation but, that is reflected in the price for a house in this location,' Caroline said hastily. 'Just take a look at that view. It's a wonderful opportunity and there is plenty of land at the rear. In fact planning permission is already in place for a double-storey extension.'

The split-level nature of this property, beloved of the seventies but not to everybody's taste, was, however, entirely suited to this site. There were four bedrooms that the previous owner had used for guests complete with tiny shower rooms but they were shoddy and would have to be ripped out. In fact the whole place Angela soon realized needed re-modelling. It was daunting but she found herself unfazed by the amount of work needed, excited rather at the prospect of transforming the interior.

Caroline was chatty and trying her best to extol the virtues of the place, looking at Angela in particular for a reaction as they toured it. The large garden stretched towards a wooded area in the distance. It had once been a lovely garden and it would not take much to haul it back into shape. Angela excused herself and wandered off alone to walk up to the far boundary so that she could turn and look back at the house and the glittering waters of the bay beyond.

When she caught up with Caroline and

Barbara who were now standing in the kitchen, she caught Barbara's questioning look and rubbed her nose.

20

It was their anniversary in September and Tom had been reminded of that small fact by Melanie. She always reminded him which was just as well because, although he would never in a million years forget Angela's birthday, the wedding anniversary did sometimes pass him by.

Over the last few years ever since the win they had gone to town on their anniversary celebration, especially last year when he had taken her for a romantic trip on the Orient Express to Venice. But it had not been a success because it came right in the middle of some tough negotiations with the Spanish builders. Sean kept ringing him at all hours, interrupting every bloody thing; dinner for two, coffee in St Mark's Square, his mobile ringing even when they were in the middle of the Grand Canal in a gondola. He had fully expected him to interrupt them in bed at night, switching off the mobile of course as a precaution, but that would not put Sean off. He would find a way.

In the end an exasperated Angela turned on him.

'I'm going to throw that fucking thing in the canal,' she said.

'Don't swear.' He was shocked at her saying *that* word. Used often it lost its impact but coming from his lovely wife, a woman he still regarded as an innocent, it was doubly shocking.

'Sorry.' She waved an apologetic hand. 'But honestly, Tom, you might look as if you're enjoying it,' she had said. 'This is supposed to be a treat for both of us and you have just ignored me, spending all the time on your phone to Sean. You would think you were married to him, not me.'

'Don't exaggerate. It's just business and Sean likes to keep me up to speed with what's happening.'

She had given him a withering look.

He had done his best to save the weekend but it was too late by then for the damage was done. They had spent the remainder of it in a state of huffiness. Trying to patch things up he had offered to take her away the following weekend to anywhere she wanted; New York maybe. Calling on desperate measures, he had even offered to make the supreme sacrifice and leave his mobile behind, but she had still refused.

After that for a while he could do nothing right. His gift of horrendously expensive ear-rings was accepted coolly and he noticed that she rarely wore them so obviously she did not like them.

He was determined that this year it would be different. He had to come up with something special but he had left it a bit late and he now had a heap of brochures to look through offering last-minute short breaks to exotic destinations. And he had no idea what to buy her. He had done the diamonds to death. She had more than enough flowers around the house to kit out a florist's and he could not buy her anything to wear because women liked to choose their own clothes. It was easy in the old days because a bottle of perfume did the trick every time, something expensive that she managed to eke out until Christmas when he would buy another.

He would have to resort to asking Melanie for suggestions. His daughter was quietly driving him mad. He had not said anything about the tattoo which she had been sporting for some time now. She thought he had not noticed but he had. Nothing escaped him so far as his daughter was concerned. He had reined in his anger, but his daughter was becoming impossible and at last he was beginning to see Angela's point of view. Melanie seemed to be having an extended gap year with nothing at the end of it and she needed to snap out of it.

She needed a job and he was going to give her an ultimatum.

In three — best make it six — months time he was stopping her allowance so, if she hadn't found a job by then — tough.

★　★　★

Melanie though was not much help when it came to thinking of something different he could pull out of the bag for the anniversary present and he was beginning to panic.

Where on earth had they not been? They had done the world tour shortly after the win. Fantastic, of course, although after a while Angela had started to miss home, or what had been their home, for plans to move had been set in motion straightaway. He saw now that although the dream of living on the Kent estuary had always been top of Angela's agenda, the house he had built was not part of that dream. He had been so excited by the plans, so delighted with the lay-out that it never occurred to him that she had been less so.

She should have said.

As for the interior design, Gus had recommended Megan and he had been swayed by the reputation she had and the exorbitant cost of the work because, after all, if it cost as much as that then it must be good.

He leafed through the travel brochures but nothing caught his eye and he hastily skipped over the pages on Spain not wishing to be reminded of that fiasco.

This anniversary was beginning to assume an importance that he hadn't felt for some time because the last one had been such a disappointment for her. This had to be a new start for them, a chance to reassess their lives which had been shaken and stirred during the last five years. It felt a bit like the last chance saloon. If he didn't pull this one off then she might just leave him. That old chestnut about money not buying happiness was turning out to be true and when you handed over a couple of thousand for a piece of jewellery and did not think twice about it, it was time to look at life again and realize just what was important.

Melanie surviving that tumble down the stairs that could have killed her was important.

Making it up to Angela and making her realize just how much he loved her was important.

The rest; the house, the cars, the diamonds, the paintings were just trifles.

This anniversary was going to be the turning point. It was do or die, for if he didn't make some bloody effort he faced the devastation of her going. He could not contemplate a future without her but what the hell could he do to convince her that there *was* a future for them?

It had to be a complete surprise, something that she would never expect in a million years. But what?

21

Tom and Angela were breakfasting together. There was an uneasy truce between them, both of them trying hard to make things right again. The happiness of the first years together was gone and she wondered with a deal of sadness if it was gone forever. If so, then perhaps they could learn to make the best of what was left and if that was a slightly depressing thought that was just the way it was. People divorced, gave up, or mostly just toddled on.

She was thankful that the Sean days were well and truly over. He had made an abortive attempt to interest Tom in other things, but at last Tom had seen the light where that gentleman was concerned, even to the extent of removing two very expensive and absolutely awful paintings that had been on the wall in that man's office. Rumours had it that Sophie was expecting again and Angela could not help a small smile at that development.

One good thing was that it poured considerable doubts on her previous suspicions that Tom was seeing another woman because he seemed unconcerned that he would no longer be making the visits down to Preston. It made her feel guilty that she had suspected him in the first place. She was trying to make it up to him but it still felt as if he was holding something back.

The financial situation was nowhere near as bad as they had feared with Charles Grey coming up trumps, damping down their panic and siphoning off funds to leave them with a more than adequate monthly income so they certainly were not on their uppers. They had lost Ron and Audrey, not through sacking but through resignations. They were moving over to Northumberland to live near Audrey's mother and their resignations were accepted with regret of course but also some relief. Tom's driving ban would not last forever and until he got back his licence he would have Angela to ferry him about.

In the meantime their tightening-belts strategy was paying off and they had netted a handsome profit from the sale of some paintings. The most surprising thing was that, almost on impulse, they were going ahead with buying the house on the hill, although Barbara, in one of her fickle moods, had pulled out. Undeterred, Angela was forging ahead, relieved in a way because without Barbara breathing down her neck she would be free to do as she wanted. With a planned extension at the rear which could be their private domain, she felt sure she would be able to run the business on her own. She would do the interior design herself this time and she was hoping that Tom would agree to do the hands-on jobs. Tom was viewing all this with bemusement although he knew better than to show any doubts for this was going to be *her* project. She would learn, with some help from Moira, to rustle up a good breakfast and she would, with Malcolm's help, soon tame the garden.

She would have something to do at last and, buoyed up by all the plans, she had even persuaded Tom to do what she had wanted for some time and put their house up for sale.

Things were just that bit better between them. She was not cold-shouldering him completely in bed so that side of life was improving. They had some way to go yet before things returned to normal, before they became the couple they had been pre-win. Who were those people? Sometimes that normality, that ordinary family life they had once shared seemed a distant dream, Angela viewed it a little mistily, the hard times conveniently forgotten, through rose-tinted spectacles.

★   ★   ★

They had a cash buyer for the house, not a lottery winner, but somebody who ran an auction house in the Grange-over-Sands area, an antiques dealer of repute who strangely adored the modernity of the house, and whose partner loved swimming so the pool had been the deciding factor.

Sitting by the pool, perversely a little sad to be leaving it behind, Angela was composing a letter to Cheryl. It was two whole months since Cheryl's letter and she must be wondering what on earth was happening. The poor woman must be thinking that she would accept a 'goodbye and thank you' letter just like that. Did their correspondence for all these years count for nothing? How could she think that she would just abandon her, just like that? And what did Moira know about it? She should have trusted her own judgement where Cheryl was concerned.

She decided she would not mention to Cheryl the visit she and Moira had made to the previous address where they had met up with Uncle Charlie. She apologized for the delay in writing to her but . . . she could not think of a reasonable excuse at this point so she chose to exaggerate the effects of Melanie's accidental, or otherwise, fall down those steps. She had been out of her mind with worry, she told Cheryl, hence the delay in sitting down to write a letter. She popped extra money in the envelope to make up for it and, because she was happier about what was now happening in her life and hopeful that maybe she and Tom could look forward to mending their relationship, she told Cheryl that in future she was going to send an increased amount.

She would of course not be informing Moira of that development.

She was going to tell Tom about Cheryl. Sometime.

★   ★   ★

'You might have told me before you sold the house,' Melanie said, amazingly, coming down to breakfast at just after eight o'clock. 'What am I supposed to do?'

'Get a job,' Tom said from behind the newspaper. 'That's what girls of your age do unless they are at college.'

'A *job*?' She rounded on her mother. 'Did you hear that? As if I haven't been trying to get one for ages now? I've had at least twenty interviews so you can't accuse me of not trying.'

'We are not putting you out on the street,' Angela said, giving Tom a look. 'You can move with us into the other house.'

'That B&B hovel?'

'It's hardly that, love, but it needs so much doing to it that we're thinking of staying in a mobile home for a while until the work is finished.'

'A *caravan?*' Melanie shrieked. 'You must be joking.'

Tom put down his newspaper. 'Hang on a minute. I gave you six months last month to get yourself a job. How is it going?'

'Six months?' She pouted prettily. 'And what's going to happen if I haven't got a job in six months?'

'Your allowance is cut,' he said with a grin. 'Sorry, sweetheart, it's for your own good. You'll have to find a way of earning your own money until your trust fund comes up.'

Angela bit her lip. She knew she had been nagging him for ages to be more ruthless with Melanie, but this was going to the other extreme. It looked very much as if he actually meant it.

There was a short silence and before her eyes Angela saw the realization hit her daughter that perhaps the days of wrapping Daddy round her little finger were gone. Angela closed her eyes briefly, waiting for it, anticipating either a yelling match or tears, both of which had worked in the past.

'OK. You win, Daddy.' Calmly, Melanie sat

down at the breakfast table. 'I'll have a job by the end of the week. I've been head-hunted as a matter of fact.'

'Head-hunted?' Tom let out a laugh but Melanie was not amused. 'Who by, for Christ's sake?'

'By whom, actually.'

Angela stood up, fussing with things on the table in an attempt to defuse the situation. 'Just coffee as usual, darling?'

'I'll have a full English, please,' Melanie said with a small tight smile. 'You might as well practise on me, Mummy, if you're determined to open this ghastly B&B.'

22

Tom needed Jim's help.

He was loath to admit it but needs must. If Angela was surprised that he was suddenly going to visit Jim of all people she made no comment. He got Melanie to drive him over, counting down the days until he got his licence back.

'So what's this job then?' he asked, marvelling silently at his daughter's driving skills as she took the many bends and twists on this road around the bay with aplomb. 'Are we allowed to know? It's driving us crazy not knowing. It's nothing funny, is it?' he asked, as a vision of his beautiful little girl lap-dancing appeared. God, he could never allow that.

'Funny?' she laughed. 'I don't know what you mean, Daddy. No, it is not. Do you remember Griselda Scott from school?'

'Griselda Scott?'

'Grizzy.'

'Oh yes. Bit of a chatterbox. Wasn't her father a diplomat in India?'

'And a whole load of other places. Grizzy flew all over the world during the hols. She was terribly cool about it all. They just put her on a plane and off she went. It was no big deal.'

'You've caught up with her again?'

'She called me. She's set up an emergency private catering service. She's done the marketing, Daddy, and we have a business plan that her brother Lucas has done for us. We see our client as a working mother, extremely busy, frantically stressed, trying to juggle a beautiful home, husband, children as well as her executive position at work where she as good as runs the world. There aren't enough hours in the day and she is bordering on suicidal because she just can't find the time for all the beauty treatments she needs to fit in because she has to keep up appearances. Her stress levels are at ninety-nine point nine per cent. Any higher and she would simply explode.'

'Poor thing.'

She laughed, a delightful girlish giggle, and Tom joined in. He much preferred his daughter like this, light-hearted with her eyes sparkling with excitement.

'Watch your speed here,' he warned, as they approached a village, putting his foot on an imaginary brake although Melanie had slowed down anyway and given him a sharp exasperated glance.

She was quiet for a moment, concentrating on her driving but as soon as they were through she picked up speed and continued where she left off.

'Well, just suppose a woman like this needs a dinner party organized at the last minute and she just hasn't the time or the energy left to lift a finger then she simply calls on us. *Grizelda saves the day* and we might even call the business something like that. We can do the lot at a moment's notice; the table, the flowers, the food, the clearing up. All our client has to do is find the time to get her heels and her frock on, do her nails, get rid of the kids for the evening and she will be the kind of hostess her friends look at with amazement. And we don't mind in the least if she wants to pretend she did the lot herself. Won't it be fantastic? We will be on the edge the entire time wondering if we're going to get a call that morning or not.'

'Hmm.' Wondering whether you were going to get a call or not sounded extremely vague to him, not at all business-like and, in addition, he could see one very big snag in this scenario. 'But you can't cook, Mel,' he pointed out gently.

'I can.' She paused as she negotiated a tight uphill bend perfectly, correct gear, correct speed. 'Surely you remember that I did a cordon bleu cookery course at school in my last year.'

He did remember vaguely that there had been one subject — the non-academic variety — about which she had received reasonable comments. Why hadn't they picked up on that? He thought she had lost interest because so far as he knew she had never even switched the oven on at home.

'Grizzy is in charge of everything *but* the cooking. She's been trying to find someone she can work with for ages and was getting desperate and then she remembered that I had a natural flair for it . . . '

Tom smiled a little. You couldn't fault his little girl for her confidence.

'So that's going to be my baby. And, after all my travels, I have picked up some super ideas about menus.'

He would take her word for it.

'I've already got five basic menus organized so that we can offer a choice. Grizzy's getting all the flyers printed and sent off and I'm moving in with her at the end of the month so I won't be in your hair any longer. She has this super apartment in Chelsea that she shares with Lucas. You needn't worry, Daddy; I have no designs on him whatsoever so I won't be bunking in with him.'

'That never occurred to me,' he said,

surprised at the comment, but pleased that she could quite obviously take care of herself these days. After all she was approaching nineteen and it was time she left the awkward teens behind. He wanted nothing more than she be happy. However, he felt it necessary to strike a note of caution. 'I'm just a little concerned, darling. It's quite ambitious for two eighteen year olds,' he said, regretting that he was coming over as middle-aged and over-cautious, thinking also that he had some room to talk as his own attempts at business had been spectacularly disastrous. 'Has she any qualifications in anything?'

'This and that,' Melanie said airily. 'The thing is she has connections which is much more important. Her mother Lady Rowena knows *everybody* and she is going to pass the word round.'

He had severe doubts, but who was he to scupper her sudden excitement? They wanted her to be enthusiastic about something and it seemed, looking at her, that she was. Good for Grizzy for touching a nerve and getting Melanie motivated at last, although perhaps it was something to do with the threat he had made, one he was not convinced he would have taken to the wire.

'So this could be a big success?' he went

on, catching her mood. 'The sky's the limit. I hope it does really well, Mel.'

'Thanks. I know you all think I'm incredibly thick.'

'No, no.' He was astonished and hurt that she should think such a thing. 'Your mother and I know that you're far from thick. You're just lazy, love, if I'm honest.'

'Maybe.' For a minute she was silent and then she said something that surprised him. 'But no more. I have something to prove to Louisa, Daddy. My clever little cousin Louisa who's going to be a doctor.'

He noted the bitterness in her voice, but did not ask any more questions. He had guessed there was something going on there, something that Angela knew about but was for some reason keeping from him.

He hoped that what he had planned for their anniversary in a week's time would really strike a nerve with Angela and make her realize that despite all the problems of late he still loved her.

'Do you think she'll be pleased?' he had asked Moira when they spoke on the phone, snatching the opportunity when Angela was out. 'You don't think it's a crap idea? It's not going over the top, is it?'

'I think she'll be thrilled, Tom. It's a lovely idea and I just hope it comes off.'

'I know. I should have thought of it ages ago.'

'Jim would never think of such a thing, not in a million years.'

If he detected a wistful note in her voice he did not say anything.

Jim loved that woman more than anything in the world and she was a fool if she didn't know it.

*　*　*

'Nearly there.' A few miles further on, Melanie glanced at him. 'Can I ask you a question, Daddy?'

'Go on.'

'Why are you selling the house? Are you in trouble financially?'

'A little. I lost money when the Spanish thing crashed, but we'll get over it. The truth is your mother never liked the house and I think she'll be a lot happier in the smaller one.'

'But you're only going to have part of it to live in,' Melanie protested. 'You're just going to have an annexe to call your own and the rest of it will be for the guests. It is downsizing gone mad.'

'What more do we need?' He grinned as they turned at last into Woodland. 'Now that you're going, Mel, we'll be on our own, just the two of us.'

'Great.'

He thought he detected a faint edge of sarcasm, but maybe he was imagining it this time. They were approaching Woodland and, as always, he experienced that little twinge of nostalgia as they passed the first of the houses on the perimeter. It had been Angela's dream, not his, to move across the bay just as it had been his dream, not hers, to live in a spanking new build.

Why on earth hadn't they talked to each other?

* * *

'Louisa's out,' Moira said, welcoming them. 'Come on in. Do you want a cup of coffee or anything before you set off again? Jim's nearly ready. He's been at the house he's doing up this morning and he's just having a shower.'

She accepted a kiss, triple continental cheek to cheek from Melanie, and a brief hug from Tom. It was getting easier, she reflected, taking them into the lounge to wait for Jim. She had always known Tom loved Angela and what he was planning now was really the proof of it and if Angela didn't realize it then she was more of a fool than she thought.

To prove she was well and truly over him, she chose to sit beside him on the sofa. To her annoyance there was still a little fizzle there and she supposed regretfully that it would always be, though she felt much more in control now. She had gone over the scenario in her head enough times and come to the conclusion that there was no way she was throwing away what she had with Jim for a one-night physical thrill.

Tom Ross was one hundred per cent out of bounds.

He seemed preoccupied and opposite them Melanie was obviously relieved that Louisa was out. Her being out was deliberate, Moira knew that, but she had not questioned it. Those two girls had a lot of thinking to do about each other.

'I hope there won't be any problems,' Tom muttered. She smiled as she saw the concern in his face. 'And I hope to God if all goes well that Jim will get over on time on Friday morning. If he doesn't turn up first thing it won't bloody well work. I'm taking her breakfast in bed and I want him there right after that.'

'Breakfast in bed?' Moira smiled. 'Wow. You are pushing the boat out. Stop worrying, Jim will be there. He was your best man, remember, and didn't he get you to the church on time? If he can do that, he can do this. By the way, how is the house purchase? Have you signed up yet?'

'We'll be in by the end of next month. You should see Angela. She's full of it and I think . . . ' — he glanced at her — 'I think she's working up to asking you for advice with the decorating.'

'Is she? I'll help all I can, of course.'

She wondered if Angela had yet told Tom about Cheryl. She had clammed up on that situation but Moira knew damned well that she had relented and was still at it, still writing the letters and, worse, still sending her money. What was the point of asking for advice and then ignoring it? Moira would put money on something being wrong with the Cheryl business although she could not put her finger on what exactly it might be.

'Don't you dare give her a hint about this,' she warned Tom sensing his nervousness. 'I've lied through *my* teeth when I spoke to her so keep quiet. We want this to be a lovely surprise for her.'

'Thanks, Moira. You've been great.'

'No problem.' She reached over, gently touched his hand. Just testing, she told herself, pleased that the gesture was just that; a friendly gesture. She was relieved however when she heard Jim coming downstairs.

'Tom!' Jim fired himself into the room at full tilt, rubbing his hands with expectation. 'Come on, you sentimental sod, let's get this thing on the road.'

'The best of luck,' she murmured to their retreating backs.

This little scheme of Tom's was all about the past, re-living it a little and, although she sometimes wondered about the dangers attached to that — worried about the rose-tinted view she sometimes had of the past herself, how she conveniently shelved the bad memories — it was the thought that counted and this time, if he could pull it off, Tom had got it exactly right.

23

'Thank heavens for that,' Melanie said, when the men were gone. 'I've never seen Daddy in such a state. He's got a bag full of cash on him. You'd think he was putting in a bid for the Crown Jewels.'

'It means a lot to him, Mel. I know he's left it all to the last minute, but if he can pull it off it will mean a lot to your mother, believe me.'

'If you say so.' She shrugged and then, with a glint in her eye, leaned forward. 'Can I tell you about *my* plans, Aunty Moira?'

She listened, marvelling that it had taken somebody like Griselda to stir Melanie up into doing something and, if sheer enthusiasm would do it then it sounded as if it might work and she said as much.

'Thanks. Dad sounded very sceptical but then he doesn't think I can do anything, but I'll show him.'

'And if it doesn't work out you've always got your money to fall back on when you're twenty-five,' Moira reminded her, wishing she hadn't because it sounded mean spirited and she hadn't meant it to. 'That was very sensible of your parents to put that aside for you.'

'For Adele and Louisa too, don't forget.'

'As if I could. It's a godsend for Louisa and will help her get started when she's finished the course.' She hesitated, wondering if she should bring up the subject that was still bothering her. 'I . . . Louisa thinks the world of you, you know that. You're like a sister to her, Mel, and I'm sure that if she did anything at all to make you doubt that . . . ' She struggled for the right words. She did not want to spell it out, not as such, but she did not want this thing, this alleged pushing-down-stairs thing, to form a barrier between them for ever.

'It's forgotten.' Melanie who had been delving into her enormous Italian leather bag snapped the clasp shut. 'Please don't mention it again because I won't.' She stood up and Moira did the same for they had things to do and she was intending to take Melanie over to visit her grandmother as promised.

The subject was closed. She wanted to say an awful lot more but instead she opened her arms and gave her niece a hug which Melanie a little self-consciously returned. Like her own daughter, there was a little trembling there but, unlike Louisa, this girl was too thin, a bag of bones, although she did not

311

think there was anything to worry about. She had always been slim and she was reminded of Melanie the little girl and her ever sturdy Louisa. Louisa, even though she was younger, had always been the one who had looked after her cousin, protective of her in a way that had made the two mothers smile, but for some time past it seemed that Louisa had been harbouring resentment towards her. Perhaps it was the weight thing although Louisa didn't seem particularly concerned or perhaps it was the unfair distribution of a breathless sexy beauty because Melanie possessed that in droves, or maybe that young man Terry had meant more to Louisa than she was letting on.

Whatever the reason, she had to let it go.

★ ★ ★

Angela was happier than she had been for years. She would be sorry to leave the garden, but gardens were fleeting things and she had plans for the new one which she would work on over the winter.

She was leaving most of the furniture in the house because the new owners loved it all and in any case they were going to have considerably less space at the new property. In the meantime until the extension was

312

finished and the renovation work completed, they would be living a doll's house existence in a mobile home on site.

They would be living in close proximity which she was well aware could make or break their tender relationship but things seemed better these days. Not perfect, but then had they ever been that? Melanie was excited about this job in London and, although like Tom Angela had reservations about it she was hoping it would work out. Perversely though, now that Melanie was actually going to move away, something she had wanted her to do for ages, she was feeling a pang to be losing her.

Things were moving quickly with the house purchase because it was cash all the way in every direction so there were no boring and long-winded mortgage applications to wait for and she couldn't wait to move into the dinky little caravan and watch the renovations taking place in the new house.

Tom was excited, too, and less upset about leaving his beloved new build than she thought he would be. It was no earthly use dwelling on the money they had lost this past year — put it down to experience — but they would not be making any more mistakes. She had not yet told him about writing to Cheryl and the money she was sending her, and she was no longer sure of the wisdom of confessing as much. Confessions, she had learnt to her cost, were sometimes best held back and what harm was it doing? Cheryl was her own private little charity and not one she cared to shout about.

★ ★ ★

It had worked.

The letters and the money were still coming. There had even been a small increase which Cheryl had been delighted to accept. Cheryl was busy settling into her new home and telling Angela all about it.

As the letters were going to a new address it meant that the visits to Uncle Walter were no longer necessary. Colin felt a surprising guilt at dropping the old bugger completely so he still popped round from time to time and helped out with the bills. Sitting with him one day at the kitchen table over a meal of steak and kidney pie — the frozen variety — roast spuds — also frozen — to be followed by a tin of Ambrosia rice pudding, Colin finally flipped and told him what it was all about.

'I thought she looked as if she had money,' Uncle Walter said, taking it all in as he demolished the pie. 'Poor sod. That's taking

314

advantage of a lonely woman, Colin.' He grinned suddenly, a blob of gravy on his chin. 'Bloody clever though.'

'She's getting her life back together,' Colin said, strangely pleased that it was working out for her. After all, he had developed an affection for the woman after all this time for hadn't she helped him to furnish his apartment with the sort of things he loved; good quality stuff, none of your chain-store rubbish. His flat was in a classy neighbourhood and although he kept himself to himself, if pressed he told people that his lowly job in the bookshop was just something to provide him with background material for the book he was writing. If pressed further he made vague mutterings about a private income. The truth was Stephen had never stopped loving him, even though he was now in a civil partnership with another bloke. That bloke would not be best pleased if he knew about the regular generous cheque coming Colin's way which meant it would continue to come along for the foreseeable future and that, together with his earnings from the bookshop and his little offering from Angela gave him a comfortable income.

He tipped the dishes in the sink, wondering if he should treat Uncle Walter to a dishwasher although it might be better to spend some money on the house itself. One of these days when the old boy popped his clogs this house would be his and he would do it up and let it out to students so it was in his best interests to start the process of tidying it up now although he wouldn't be doing any large-scale work in that backyard in case he disturbed anything or anybody.

'Angela's moving house,' he said, watching Uncle Walter eating his rice pudding. 'She's setting up a B&B business. I might book in sometime,' he added as the thought struck him. 'She won't have a clue who I am and it will be nice to meet her face to face. What do you think about that idea?'

Uncle Walter grinned. 'You're a head case,' he said proudly.

24

Angela had no idea what Tom was doing over at Moira's although she was pleased that the two men seemed to be growing up at last and putting aside their differences. It was just that he had never before visited of his own doing, always dragged along by her so it was something of a mystery.

'Not a clue,' Moira had said when she phoned her. 'Maybe Jim's persuaded him to try fishing. You know Jim's always been keen.'

'I can't see Tom fishing. He's much too fidgety.'

'It's male bonding stuff,' Moira said with a laugh. 'It's the equivalent of our pampering session.' There was a pause before she asked about their forthcoming wedding anniversary. 'Do you want me to remind him? You know what these men are like for remembering dates.'

'Melanie usually reminds him but thanks anyway.'

It was lucky Moira had reminded *her* in fact because with the house move and everything it might easily have passed unnoticed. After the fiasco last year, she was in no mood for another disaster and hoped to goodness he was not planning anything outrageous. He was apt to go daft when it came to travel and the last thing she wanted was a long weekend in China or somewhere equally far flung. Nor did she need any more diamonds and if that was ridiculous then that could not be helped. She loved her jewellery — what woman wouldn't? — but funnily enough the one item in the jewellery box that she really treasured was the silver bangle he had given her after they had been going out together for a few months.

It had been her birthday and things at home were tense because Moira was still smarting from Tom's rejection. Still, that could not dampen Angela's anticipation as she waited for him to appear. She knew Moira was peeping from the upstairs window, but she could not help that and her heart gave a little excited leap as she saw or rather heard the sound of his car coming down the road. That car had done them proud, a pale blue Beetle of which he was inordinately fond. It was noisy and uncomfortable and he called it Sheila, urging her up the hills when she threatened to slow down to a stop. The stuttering progress was immensely irritating for those following, but who cared? He liked living on the edge, Tom told her, who the hell

318

wanted a car that was *reliable*, for Christ's sake?

He drove her to Blackpool where they spent the rest of the day. She had known him a little while only but if there had been a defining moment she fell in love with him on that day.

★ ★ ★

It was not far into the New Year and cold.

There was something about the resort in winter that appealed to her much more than the brazen bustle of the summer months. The place was almost deserted and the few people who were around were wisely not risking walking along the lower walk of the promenade on the north shore because the waves were at full force, hitting the sea wall with a ferocity that sent spray far and wide so that, even at a safe distance, they were still bombarded with a light dusting of it. That and the sea breeze were ruining her hair, her make-up, but she couldn't care less for Tom was beside her, holding her hand and laughing. They had talked and talked and never before had she felt so at ease as it dawned that here was the man with whom she would spend the rest of her life.

At last as it began to rain properly they

took cover in the shelter of one of the colonnades parking themselves on the dry bench. She wished now she had accepted her mother's offer to bring along a flask of coffee but that had seemed like a middle-aged thing to do and in any case Tom had other ideas. He drew her to him roughly, their coats smelling of damp, their faces nipped with the cold, their eyes shining. With nobody about he kissed her, tilting her face and gently stroking her cheek so that time stood still a moment and that moment, like the rest of that day, was to be locked in her memory for ever. Leaning against him, she closed her eyes, listening to the sound of the angry waves, the soaring seagulls and smelling and tasting the saltiness of the air.

'Happy birthday, sweetheart,' he said, producing a prettily wrapped package from his pocket and, as he passed it over, he whispered the treasured words for the first time telling her that he loved her. It was too soon, much too soon, and she remembered thinking of Moira and how she would react to this but it was all too late for she too loved *him*.

Packing up her jewellery now in readiness for the move, Angela picked up the silver bangle and placed it round her wrist with a smile. She rarely wore it these days but in an odd way it meant more than the engagement ring that was to appear much later and considerably more than the costly diamond ring that he bought her after the win. One day the bangle would go to Melanie as would all of it but she knew that Melanie would never wear it, that it would lay tossed aside in the box for it was altogether too cheap and simple for her darling daughter.

Briskly, she replaced it in the box. This was no time for sentiment. She had things to do. They might only be moving up the road and taking few possessions with them but what they were taking needed to be packed away and stored. Eventually they would be opening up three rooms for guest occupation, each of which would have its own en suite. Downstairs the guests would have the use of a lounge and dining-room. Moira would help with the décor and she was aiming for traditional good taste coupled with a dash of the unexpected.

Excitement bubbled up. At last she had something to get her teeth into again.

★ ★ ★

Angela enlisted Melanie's help in choosing a new dress. She had had a root around but could not find any air tickets so she suspected

Tom was keeping it simple this time and just taking her out for dinner which suited her fine. She wanted something new to wear, something to signify the new chapter in their lives that was coming like it or not. With Melanie soon to be out of the picture and the move pending as well it was the perfect moment for reassessment of their relationship.

'Wait until you see what he's got planned for your anniversary,' Melanie said, shooting her a sly glance as she parked outside the boutique.

'I hate surprises,' Angela said. 'He's not doing something daft, is he? I hope he's not been talking to Moira. Has he?'

'Might have,' her daughter said obviously dying to tell her.

A thought hit her suddenly. 'Oh for heaven's sake, I hope we're not renewing our vows. I know she thinks it's wonderful ever since she went to her friend's do last year so she might have put that idea in his head. It's just like her.'

'And what's wrong with that?' Melanie said, worryingly not denying it. 'Don't be so miserable, Mum. I think it's a lovely idea.'

'Maybe it is for some people but not for us. If he's dragging me over to the church in Woodland he can forget it and if the whole family is in on it then I will kill him. We do not *need* to reaffirm our vows. Once is enough for anybody,' she said, with so much feeling that Melanie laughed and after a moment so did Angela. 'Sorry,' she added. 'I just don't want to go through that palaver again.'

'Palaver?' Melanie slipped her arm through hers, a nice and unexpected gesture. 'Honestly, Mum, I despair of you sometimes, I really do.'

Melanie looked youthful and happy today and Angela could not believe the transformation, was almost waiting for the bubble to burst and for Melanie to revert to her normal unhelpful self. However, looking at her and seeing that she was dying to let her in on the secret only confirmed that, nudged into the idea by Moira, Tom *was* planning a huge celebration with her at the centre of it, the two of them standing in St Andrew's church renewing their vows.

She smiled anyway, loving the sound of her daughter's laughter. Whatever the reason, the kick up the backside by Tom, or the stirring into action by the effervescent Grizzy, it was welcome. And yes, she did want her to succeed even though she recognized that part of it was to do with proving something to Louisa who was not quite as perfect as the rest of the family liked to think.

25

Angela sensed Tom up and about early and was very nearly drifting off again when she heard the door opening, the breakfast tray rattling followed by a curse as he presumably stubbed his toe on the bed-post.

Reluctantly, she raised herself to a sitting position catching sight of her bleary-eyed self, hair a complete mess, in the dressing table mirror. Her nightdress had slithered off her shoulder as she struggled to sit up but the resulting baring of her breast was comical rather than sexy. Quickly she hoisted the strap back into position noting that there was a single pink rose and an anniversary card sitting on the tray as well as orange juice, coffee, her low-fat, low-taste cereal, whole-meal toast, cholesterol-busting margarine and marmalade.

'Good morning, my darling, and happy anniversary,' Tom said drawing the curtains back so that the morning light flooded into the room making her squint at the sudden brightness. It looked like a perfect day. The sky was blue, the waters of the bay silvery and twinkling, the golden sands sweeping into the distance with never a hint of the danger lurking there; quick-sands that had been known to suck down a horse and cart, treacherous tides that craftily sneaked up on you. All they needed was a shark off shore and they would have the lot.

'Happy anniversary,' she echoed, lifting her face for his kiss and resisting the urge to add that she hoped it would be better than last year.

'Freshly squeezed orange juice, your crap cereal, toast toasted to perfection and some of Annie's homemade marmalade. We still have two jars left.'

'Audrey,' she corrected him. 'I must drop them a line, see how they're getting on and tell them about our move.'

'Yes. Remember me to Ron. Do you want anything else? I can do a fry-up if you want.'

'No, thanks. Although you will have to learn how to do a proper breakfast when we're running the business in case you need to step in.'

'No problem.' He winked at her and suddenly looked twenty years old again. 'I'll ask for instructions from our very own cordon-bleu chef before she departs.'

They smiled at each other and she patted the bed for Tom to sit near her. 'I hear from Melanie that you've got a surprise for me,' she said. 'I hope I've got something suitable to wear, whatever it is. Oh Tom . . . ' She poured the skimmed milk onto the cereal. 'I think I know what it is. We're renewing our vows, aren't we?' She tried hard to quell the sudden panic in her voice. 'Will everybody be there? All the people who were at our wedding? I can't believe you've done this. Whose idea was it? No, don't tell me, it was Moira, wasn't it? She's always wanted to do it so I can't believe she's going to be pleased that I've beaten her to it so that's going to cause no end of problems. And what the hell am I supposed to wear? I'm not expected to squeeze back into my wedding dress, am I?'

'Hey, stop panicking.' He seemed momentarily confused. 'Where does Moira fit into this? I've no idea where you got all this from but you've totally got the wrong end of the stick. It never occurred to me that you would want to do that. *Do* you want to do it because if so you're going to be very disappointed?'

'No, of course I don't,' she said, sitting up properly and reflecting that, nice gesture as it was, breakfast in bed was a highly over-rated business although she would not dream of telling him. Crumbs got *everywhere*.

'We don't need to renew our vows anyway,' he went on, still puzzled. 'Once is enough surely?'

Finishing off her breakfast, she could see that he was on edge, back at the window again, looking out and then she heard the sound of a car coming up the drive, a distinctive engine noise that most certainly did not belong to either of theirs.

She knew what it was immediately.

'Good God, Tom, what have you done?'

Jumping out of bed, clattering the dishes on the tray, she ran over to the window. There it was, shuddering to a halt with Jim stepping out of the driving seat a minute or two later.

'It's Sheila,' she exclaimed, and there was no need to confirm it by reading the number plate. 'Where did you find her?'

'It's a long story,' he said, putting his arm round her. 'We've Jim to thank for tracing it for us. He knew the bloke we originally sold it to and he told him who he had sold it on to and we were bloody lucky that he still lived in the area. Are you cold?'

'Not a bit,' she said, although the window was open and the morning bay air, always faintly chill, was slipping into the room. 'Have you bought or borrowed it?'

'Bought,' he told her. 'He didn't want to sell because he'd spent money doing it up. He never used it and it's just sat in the garage for the last ten years. It pained him to sell but he changed his mind when I told him he could

327

name his price — within reason that is and we came to an agreement. It doesn't matter how much. Don't ask. But I thought we should start afresh, go back to the old days and this seemed as good a way as any. Get your glad rags on and I'll . . . or rather Jim . . . will take us for a spin. Unless you want to have a go at driving it . . . ' He eyed her anxiously. 'You never did drive it, did you?'

'I didn't have a licence then. I'd love to drive it,' she said, staying close. Jim had looked up at the window and given them a cheery wave and, mindful of her diaphanous nightgown, she stepped back. Now, out of Jim's view, she drew Tom towards her so that she could kiss him in private, a proper kiss that should leave him in no doubt whatsoever that they were back on track. 'This is the best present ever, darling,' she whispered, slipping her arms round his neck and looking into his eyes. They had, she realized, not really been this close in a while, close in every sense and even as she contemplated the dizzy delights of driving the little old car, she felt the years spinning and as he drew her even closer for another breath-defying kiss, they were back to the beginning.

Young, daft and in love.

★   ★   ★

Angela was doing a practice run for the B&B.

Her guests this weekend were Jim and Moira who would be in one of the double guest rooms and her mother Dilys who would be staying in the single room. It had taken some time to get things as they wanted and Christmas had come and gone in some confusion as the renovations were not completed. Moira had suggested they come over to them for Christmas but in the event they had gone down to London meeting up with Melanie who was enjoying her new independence. Her youthful excursions into private catering with her energetic friend Grizzy seemed to be working out although they both became vague when money matters were mentioned.

Angela was going to leave them to it. She had control now of the purse-strings in their house and wondered why on earth she had ever let go of them. Tom was much happier doing the practical stuff and he had been a huge help in overseeing the painting and decorating. The house on the hill which they renamed Fortune Cottage was now a delight and even the garden, her speciality, was starting to come into its own and by the summer should be a magical place.

'Treat us just as you would your guests,' Dilys said, coming up the path assisted by

Moira who seemed concerned that she might slip on the slate slabs. 'Pretend we're real people not family.'

Moira laughed at that but it was what Angela wanted to do anyway and she dutifully got Tom to help with the bags and showed them to their rooms.

'No smoking, Mother,' Angela said, leaving her to have a rest in the pretty single room. Knowing her mother, Angela had turned the heat up so that it was like a little oven.

'I know that,' she grumbled. 'You can't smoke anywhere these days. As a matter of fact I'm seriously considering giving up. You can get these patches which help with the craving.'

★ ★ ★

'I can't see that happening,' Moira said once they were back downstairs and she was admiring the new lay-out of the sitting-room with the big bay window giving spectacular views of the sands and sea. 'And in a way I don't think I can put up with her if she gives it up. Life won't be worth living and I'd rather she dies happy.' She glanced at Angela. 'Is everything OK with you two?'

'Absolutely. We've turned things round, Moira. This is just what we needed. Last time the change was forced on us but this time . . . ' She hesitated, not sure how to put it. 'This is our doing. This is our choice this time. And we're not skint by any means. We've gone through a lot of money but that's life, isn't it? Melanie's a lot happier, too, so it can't be bad.'

'Thank God for that.' Moira sighed. 'I was worried for a while there that you were going to do something stupid and leave him. Buying you that Beetle was an inspiration, wasn't it?'

'Was that his idea or yours?' Angela glanced at her, remembering that Moira had always had a thing for the Beetle just as she had for Tom. 'It doesn't matter. It was a lovely thought. How's Louisa?' she asked after a moment's hesitation. 'Is she enjoying the course?'

'She's fine. Very busy. Single-minded. Men are out of the equation she tells me. I think she'll make a good doctor.' Her own hesitation was minimal. 'She's learned a lot about herself this last year, Angie. We're not perfect by any means and we all have our cross to bear and sometimes we do things that surprise us but — '

'Don't go there.' Angela shook her head, knowing what she was referring to. It would never quite be forgotten, she knew that, but given time it would be submerged into the family subconscious, one of those things never mentioned, one of those little secrets that families keep to themselves.

'What's happened to Cheryl?' Moira pulled herself out of her temporary melancholy and smiled. 'Don't tell me you're still sending her money?'

'Ssh.' Angela glanced round anxiously. 'I couldn't abandon her but I'm not going to see her, Moira. We decided that would be a mistake.'

'Who decided? You or her?'

'Both of us.' She glanced round but Tom was nowhere around. 'I might tell him but I don't think he would get it. So . . . ?'

'My lips are sealed.' Moira plumped up the cushions behind her and smiled. 'This is a lovely room, Mrs Ross. The view is fantastic.'

Angela saw she was role-playing. 'Would you like tea or coffee, Mrs Rayner?'

'That would be lovely. Coffee, please.'

'Coming up. There are magazines in the rack for you to look at and leaflets on the hall table for things to do in the area,' she said briskly, relishing her landlady mode. 'And later, I can recommend several restaurants for your evening meal. Do take a key when you go out. Breakfast tomorrow is in the dining room from seven thirty. May I wish you a very pleasant stay.'

Within months Tom had his licence back and whenever they could they took the Beetle out for a Sunday afternoon drive just as they had in the old days. They went to Blackpool, just the once, for old times' sake, choosing a cold clear day and taking that same stroll along the lower promenade walk along the north shore.

It was windy and the high spring tide was whipped into frenzy, the sound of the waves tumultuous, the whole experience exhilarating as the spray shot upwards and over the wall, raining down and drenching them. The famous tower loomed in the distance, lights vaguely twinkling, a constant reminder of where they were.

'If somebody had told us all those years ago that it would have turned out like this we would never have believed them,' Tom said, looking happier than he had done for years. 'Rags to riches, not many people have that.'

'It was hardly rags and we didn't really know for a long time what to do with the riches,' she said, swinging hands with him and knowing that the tough times were over and that, whatever happened in the future, they were fully equipped to face it. 'And neither did Melanie. Thank goodness she came through it in the end although it was a tough call.'

'Moira and Jim seem OK too, don't they?'

'They're fine.' She shot him a glance. 'She's over you now.'

'I don't know what you're talking about,' he huffed.

She laughed. 'Oh yes you do.'

'Your hands are cold.'

They paused and Tom took hold of both her hands, rubbing warmth into them. It was such an affectionate thing to do that she wanted to fall against him and cuddle into him but, because another couple were approaching, she made do with a smile instead. Once they reached the nearest colonnade they ducked into it for shelter. Cold and damp with pools of muddy water underfoot, overwhelmingly concrete and very likely used for dubious purposes these days out of the way and hidden as it was, it was hardly the place for lovers. Nobody was around though and, seizing the moment, Tom kissed her now as he had kissed her then. Bundled up as they were, their faces and particularly their noses were cold and yet it managed to be one of the most romantic things he had done in ages, kissing her here as if it was for the first time, and even though it was so familiar it was also thrilling and almost a new experience.

'It was here on this very spot,' she said quietly. 'That you first told me you loved me. Remember?'

'Of course I do. Would I forget something like that? I even remember what you were wearing.'

'I don't believe that for a minute, Tom Ross,' she teased. 'You don't even remember what I was wearing yesterday.'

The squally weather had produced a sudden sharp shower which looked as if it was the prelude to more persistent rain. Visibility had closed in so that they could hear the surge of the sea but scarcely see beyond the wall. There was little point in risking pneumonia, so they abandoned the shelter and made a run for it back to the car.

'We'll come back here for our ruby wedding,' Tom called out. 'Is that a date?'

'You bet.'

It was an interesting experience going for a trip in Sheila because of her temperamental nature and her stubborn insistence on not always doing what was expected of her but they were in the AA and they would come to their rescue if necessary. In any case, it added an edge to the experience.

Tom started the engine which after a

g moment spluttered noisily to life,
ring 'Thank God' as it did so. Beside
Angela giggled. What on earth were they
aying at? At home, Tom's luxurious Jaguar
and her own highly dependable car were in
the garage, both of which would have given
them a much smoother ride and an absolute
guarantee of getting home.

But, after all they had been through, she
was happy enough to take her chances.

THE END